Finally Home

Laura Temp

Contents

1

The small black car pulled up to the gate of the ranch and started to drive up.

"Stop here." I spoke up to the driver. He stopped and I got out. I slung my duffle over my shoulder and started walking up the long driveway.

It was a cold October and my uniform wasn't keeping me very warm. I was still use to Afghanistan's desert heat.

I looked around me and soaked in the Montana view. One I had missed for eight years now. I took off into the army when I turned 18 and stayed for three deployments. One in Korea, two in Afghanistan. My father didn't exactly approve of me leaving but he always said he was proud to have another child serve in the military. My last tour just ended early and no one knew I was coming home. Home to stay.

I could see the cabin when Kayce stepped onto the porch. He had a mug in his hand. He didn't see me at first but when he did, he glanced twice. I could see his smile and it made me smile. He turned around and went inside.

"Hey! Mary's here!" I heard him yell then the screen door slam.

He basically just off the porch then jogged in my direction. I started running to him, realizing how much I missed everyone.

"Kayce." I inhaled as I wrapped my arms around his neck.

"Hey little sister." He kissed the top of my head. "God, you've changed so much." He looked back at me then pulled me back into a hug.

He was embracing me when I heard Beth.

"Mary?!" She cried and started towards us. She had part of her make up on and hair still in rollers.

"Beth!" I meet her halfway and almost knocked her down in a hug.

"I fucking hate you." She mumbled and squeezed me tight.

"I know." I squeezed my eyes shut tight. When I opened them, Daddy was standing on the porch.

I let go of Beth and walked slowly to him. Slowly up the stairs until I was face to face.

"I'm home, Dad." I swallowed hard. Pushing the lump out of my throat.

He nodded and looked down at the ground. "Yeah." He grunted. Then he sniffled.

"Daddy." I whispered as I wrapped my arms around his neck.

He held me for a second then pat my back and stepped away. "Good timing, kid. We've got work to do."

He cleared his throat then stepped inside. Beth walked past me. "Went better than I thought."

Kayce slung his arm around me and chuckled,"Me too." I leaned into him. "I bet you're ready to be outta that uniform." He nudged me forward and we stepped into our childhood.

"Ready for eight years." I chuckled and started upstairs into my old room.

It was the same as when I left it. Down to the George Strait CD laying on my desk. No one even listens to CDs. I dropped my duffle and opened my old closet. Hopefully something still fits.

I pulled out an old pair of wranglers and slipped them on. A little tight, but they'll do for now. I grabbed a thermal shift, a long sleeve shirt, a sweatshirt and a vest. I put them all on, layer by layer. Then I tied my bandana around my neck and stuffed it into my clothes. I glanced around my room. My tan cowboy hat still hung on the wall. It was still covered in dirt and scuffs and marks. I picked it up and smiled.

I'm home. With dad and Kasey and Beth.

I put the hat on then started back down stairs and out the back door. I took the long walk to the bunk house.

My boots clinked as I stepped into the concrete floor barn.

A cowboy stood beside the saddles. He was replacing the straps on one. His black cowboy hat covered his face completely. He wore a bulky black Carhartt coat and wrangler jeans with spurs in the backs of his boots. I stared at him for a minute. I almost walked by, not realizing who he was. I almost asked him where the man was that I was looking for. But it was him. He was a changed person. There was a quietness to him. Some mysteriousness something. He looked way different. He looked even more rough and ragged than when I left. Something had happened. A lot of things had happened while I was gone.

"Hey, cowboy." I called out to Rip as I walked up to him.

He turned quickly and squinted his eyes. The morning sun was behind me and he struggled to see who I was at first. Then he realized.

"I'll be damned." He huffed. "Come here."

I smiled wide and slung my arms around his neck and squeezed tightly. He wrapped his arms around my waist and back and held me tightly as well.

I pulled back and grabbed his face with my hand. "Damn, a full beard." I tugged on it. He chuckled and pushed me away. "Looks like you finally put some weight on too. Ya look good." I thumped his chest. "I barely recognized you."

"All right now, easy." He shook his head and smiled down at me. Something I rarely ever got to see from him. His smile faded and we were soon just staring at each other. "How are you?" He asked lowly. He knew.

I opened my mouth to speak then closed it. And just nodded. He nodded as well just a seriousness in his eyes.

"Mary?" Lloyd peaked around the corner.

"Hey!" I made my way to Lloyd.

"My god, you've gotten old." He hugged me for a second.

I chuckled and shook my head. "Speak for yourself, old man. I was told there was work to do. Where are we starting?"

*****

I did wrangler work that week and enjoyed it. I enjoyed being away from the politics and puzzles that my father was involved in. I definitely enjoyed being out of the Army. As much as I loved it, it took a toll on my life.

Be a wrangler wasn't easy. I forgot how hard of work it was. And it was cold. So cold.

We were sorting through the calves when I noticed ones eye was glossy. It had discharge around it.

"Ryan!" I hollered at him, he rode over to me.

"Yeah?" He pulled down his bandana that was around his face. I did the same.

"2481. Look like pink eye to you?" I asked.

He cursed and nodded. "I'll let Rip know."

"Don't worry about it, I'll call the vet." I headed back towards the barn. Rip was putting up a small corral.

I slowed down on my way through. "Hey I'm gonna call vet. Looks like pink eyes gonna start up soon." I hollered down to him quickly while passing by.

He had a tooth pick between his teeth. When he looked up he was pissed.

"Slow down, girl. I can't fucking understand ya."

"Whoa." I mumbled to my horse and pulled back on her reins. I turned around sharply, pissed at how he had spoken to me. "I'm calling...the vet... one of the calves... has pink eye." I said super slow.

He walked up to me and my horse. "You don't have to get smart about it. Between how fast you talk and that damn accent, ain't nobody can understand you."

I dismounted my horse and started to speak.

"What the fuck is that?" Rip asked before I say anything. He grabbed my jaw roughly. "Is that chew?" His face turned red.

I shoved his hand off my face,"Yeah, what about it?"

"No wonder I can't understand ya. You got a wad of dirt shoved in your lip." He stared at me. Getting more pissed by the second.

I spit liquid out onto the ground. That didn't help any.

"Spit it out." He grumbled.

"Rip, I'm a big girl. I can chew, fuck, smoke, and drink whenever I want." I taunted.

He released a deep breath and shook his head. He glanced back at Lloyd who looked straight to the ground. He wasn't having any part of this. Smart man. "Barn, now." Rip said a little louder and harsher, enough for me to listen.

I stomped that way with him tailing close behind him. We made our way into the barn, out of everyone's sight.

Rip pinned me up against a stall.

"The fuck are you doin'?!" I hollered as he used his forearm to hold me against the stall across my collarbone.

He grabbed my lip roughly,"Ah! Ow!" It didn't hurt bad but enough to piss me off. He scooped out the tobacco I had in my lip. "Rip!" I tried shoving him off me. He dropped his arm slightly. "Goddammit, what the hell is wrong with you?" I cursed and shoved him.

He quickly shoved me back. "Don't goddammit me, goddammit. What the hell is wrong with you? Chewing? Why would you ever start that?" He shoved me against the stall one more time then let me go.

My hand went straight to my lip. It wasn't bleeding but it hurt. "Because I shot people for a living. I needed something to help pass the time." I smarted at him.

He took a few steps back and paced back and forth. He looked everywhere but at me. Then he stopped and shoved his thumbs into his belt loops. "I don't know how you made it through the fucking army with that mouth of yours."

I small smile played on my lips. I couldn't help it. Because he wasn't wrong. "It wasn't easy. Got my ass smoked a lot because of it." I tried not to chuckle.

He shook his head,"Don't let me catch you chewing again. Got it?" He pointed at me.

I stared at him. My smile completely gone. Who the fuck was this guy?

"Got it?" He asked again, but harsher.

"Yes sir."

It was the only answer that felt appropriate since he was treating me like this.

Then he stormed out.

*****

Not long after coming home I started having nightmares. Night mares that felt so real because they were real at one time.

I crawled into bed one night and closed my eyes. I fell asleep almost immediately from the exhaustion of working today.

I drifted off into another bad memories. The worst memory.

I laid on top of the building beside a E6 rookie, Jake. We switched shifts almost 7 hours ago. I laid behind my sniper rifle and focused on keeping my breathing slow and hoped time would fly by fast with any movement in the town below us.

But within seconds there was movement. My breath caught slightly but I calmed it again.

There was a small child slipping from door frame to door frame, holding something.

I pressed the button into my radio,"Lima Alpha November Delta." I called to our land team and let them know what was going on.

"Copy." They called back.

I waited and waited and waited for a response. But nothing. The child stayed at one door, as if they heard us although I know they couldn't.

"Tango Oscar papa," Or TOP which was me, came across the radio,"It's foreign. He holding something. Can't tell what it is, over."

"Copy. What's your command, over." I spoke softly back.

Jake stirred next to me. I glanced over at him.

"Everything okay?" He whispered. I gave a nodded.

"Judgement call, Corporal, over." My radio came through. Not what I wanted to hear.

"Copy, Sarge." I choked back.

Jake closed his eyes again.

I kept an eye on the child. He looked nervous through my scope. I couldn't make out what was in his arms. I squinted heard.

Could've been a bomb or a loaf of bread, I couldn't fucking tell.

"Sarge, I need eyes." I called into him.

The child started to look around more frequently and moved door frames again.

No answer from the radio.

"Lima alpha November delta," I called to them,"Eyes. I need eyes, over." I said harsher.

Jake stirred again but didn't wake up. I wish he would.

No answer. "Sarge, over?" I called again.

Jake blinked,"What's going on?" He whispered.

"Radio silent." I whispered back while staring down at the kid. "Alpha India Romeo,"I called to our air men,"Do you have eyes on Lima alpha November delta, over."

"Negative, over." The voice was panicked.

"Fuck." I mumbled again,"Then find them." I called back.

"Copy, corporal."

Jack rolled onto his stomach and grabbed his binoculars. "Is that a kid?" He asked.

"Yeah." The kid started to move. "I'm gonna loose sight." I laid my finger in the trigger.

"It's a kid, Dutton." Jake said a little louder and panicked. He was young. Maybe 20 at most.

"Look away, private." I whispered.

He stared at me then rolled onto his back.

"Any eyes on target?" I called into the radio.

"No eyes." AIR called back. Silence from LAND.

"Tango Oscar papa. Firing." I gave the coordinates. Then release a slow breathe and aim my sniper riffle. The red dot in my scope laid on the small child chest. I resumed to between the air and stopped breathing. Then squeezed the trigger.

I barely heard the bullet because of my silencer but I watched the child fall.

Jake rolled over,"Oh god." He cupped his mouth. He was going to throw up.

"Don't you fucking dare." I mumbled,"You make a fucking noise, you blow everyone's cover. It's about to get dirty."

I waited for LAND to come in and get the body but nothing.

"Lima alpha November delta, retrieve." I called into the radio.

Nothing.

"Come in Sarge?" I said again.

I heard shuffling.

Jake looked over at me. I nodded and he grabbed his riffle. He was ready.

I kept my eye on the ground below. Then I heard more shuffling and stomping.

"This is tango Oscar papa. We need eyes. No, Bravo Uniform. Bravo uniform! Now!"

My whole world went black and all I could hear was my radio.

"Lima alpha November delta! Alpha India Romeo! Eyes! I need eyes! No no eyes! Bravo uniform! Bird! Send a bird! We're covered! Bravo uniform!" I opened my eyes and looked around. It was me. It wasn't my radio.

"Hey! Mary, you're home! You're home! Stop it you're home!" A man stood at the doorway yelling at me. I flinched and looked at him.

"Sarge?" I whispered. "We need... we need eyes..." I stared harder it not Sarge.

"Mary, it's Kayce. You're at home. You're home. In Montana. At the ranch, Mary." It was Kayce. Long hair and all. He slowly walked towards me. I nodded.

"I'm at the ranch. With you. And dad and Beth." I nodded more and breathed heavily.

"Yeah," He grabbed me and hugged me,"You're at the ranch, Mary. You're not out there anyway. You're home." He held me tight.

I rested my forehead on his chest.

"I wanted to tell you they go away but they don't." He whispered. "They just become normal."

I nodded. It wasn't what I wanted to hear.

"Get some sleep." He kissed the top of my head and let me go. He walked out.

And I was stuck standing alone. In a quiet room I could hear Kayces footsteps down the hall.

I laid down but couldn't sleep.

So I got up.

2

I slipped on my work clothes and walked quietly down stairs. It was 3:30am. No one would be up for another hour or so.

The air was cold outside. I pulled my bandana over my nose to keep my face warm.

I made my way down to the barns. I looked down the where the colts are. The ones that needs to be broke. And the other barn where the ones are ready to ride. Then there was the bunkhouse. It was silent. No one would be awake until 6 here. I glanced up on the hill. Rips cabin porch light flipped on. He was must be awake.

I smiled then walked over to start feeding the horses. When I was finished I cleaned saddles. Then I pulled a horse out of the stall and slung a saddle on him.

"You ready?" I pet his mane and jumped into the saddle.

I held the reins with my gloved hands and off we went.

I took a short ride and was back when the sun was still down. Rip was walking into the barn when I lead Conway in. I checked my watch. 4:45.

He glanced in my direction and nodded.

I pulled my bandanna down to around my neck. "Horses are already feed." I spoke up and let the horse into his stall.

"I don't feed anymore." He grunted and grabbed his saddle.

I dusted my hands off onto my jeans,"Then why are you up so early?" I closed the stable door and latched it.

He slung the saddle onto an older horse, Breaker.

"I heard wolves." He strapped the saddle in.

"At five in the morning?" I questioned and leaned against one of the stall doors.

He didn't say anything and just shoved past me.

Later that day we were checking fences. Ryan, Colby, and I found a break in the fence around pasture 9. We stopped when we found them.

Colby jumped off his horse and inspected the fence.

"It's been cut." He said.

"Cut?" Ryan questioned and jumped off his horse too. I did the same and went to looked at as well.

Sure enough, it was snapped in half.

I looked around the fence. No other cuts. Just this one. But something caught my eye. A pile of stringy brown grain.

"Is that alfalfa?" I mumbled.

"Huh?" Ryan asked.

I pointed the other said the fence, right across from the break. Then we heard a groan. I squinted and saw a glimpse of black laying down. Colby apparently saw it too.

"Oh shit." Colby started to jog to it. "Grab the bag!" He hollered.

I grabbed the medic bag from my saddle while Ryan had already been running Colbys way. A momma cow was laid over by the alfalfa. Groaning and crying. She was so swollen. I dug through the bag to find the knife. I felt the cold blade of my hand.

I froze for a second.

The sound of screaming filled my ears and the smell of burning flesh filled my nose. I felt my pistol in my hand. Felt my back against a door. A hot door with flames behind it.

A man in white robes now brown and red with blood and dirt busted through a window in front of me. I aimed and pulled the trigger multiple times. The bullet pierced him but he kept coming. I emptied my clip and didn't have time to change it. I reached in my vest and felt my knife. Cold against my hand. I pulled it out as he started to fall onto him to attack-

"Mary! Now!" I heard someone yell.

I blinked multiple times. I looked around, suddenly aware I was in the pasture with the dying momma cow.

Colby had the powder in his hand, ready to cover to wound after I puncture the stomach.

I refocused and did as I was suppose to.

I puncture the stomach and the gas emitted from her. Colby and Ryan finished working on her.

I fell back and sat in the ground. Pulling my knees to close with my arms and watched. Terrified of the flash back that had just happened. I had heard of flashbacks, but never knew if they really happened and how they felt. I looked up at the sky. Light blue covered with gorgeous fluffy clouds and framed by dark blue, snow covered mountains and trees.

"Ya alright?" Colby squatted down in front of me.

"Uh, yeah. Just, haven't had to do that for a long time." I stood up and dusted off the back of my jeans. "I'll get back to the ranch and call the vet. You wanting to stay with her? It'll be dark soon. I don't want coyotes or wolves getting to her."

"That'll work. Be careful." Ryan nodded as I took off. Him and Colby stayed behind.

I rode into the ranch like a bat outta hell. I jumped off my horse while he was basically still running. I ran into the bunk house and grabbed the phone off the wall. Then I walked around the barn and corrals, trying to find signal. It was dark now so I didn't see Rip walking towards me from his cabin.

"What's going on?" He grumbled.

"Someone cut the fence by an alfalfa patch-" I started to speak but realized he probably thought it was gibberish. By the look on his face, he definitely did. I released a deep breath and slowed down, "The fence was broken in pasture 9. One of the momma cows walked across it into a patch of alfalfa. Ate a bunch of it. We did what we can but I'm calling the vet." I check to see if I had signal. I still didn't. I started to walk around.

"Don't call the vet. Just take shifts keeping an eye on her to see if she gets up." He grabbed the phone from me.

My jaw nearly dropped. "Rip even if she ate alfalfa that calf could still be alive. Then it'll kill her if she has it. We need an ultrasound on her." I reached across the grab the phone back.

He stopped and look over at me with a dead stare,"Are you questioning me?" He grunted.

I nodded,"Yeah I am."

He looked down,"Listen, I've put up with your shit all fucking week. You've been gone for eight goddamn years. You don't know how shit works anymore. Things have changed." He turned around and started to walk away.

My blood boiled. "What's wrong with you? Why the hell are you acting like this? You're treating me like-" I walked towards him. He turned around harshly and put his finger to my chest.

"You wanna act like an wrangler? I'm gonna treat you like one. Obviously no one else is going to." He spat out.

I swallowed hard,"Is that what this is about? How the wranglers treat me?" I squinted my eyes to try and understand him under that big hat.

He was breathing heavy but didn't say anything.

I released a soft breath,"Rip, I know things have changed. And it seems like a lot happened while I was gone. But one thing hasn't changed and it's how to raise cattle. You know as well as I do that if that calf is alive in her, when she has it'll kill her and the calf. She's in early pregnancy. If the vet catches it now, we can get it out her before it poisons her." My sentences were quietly and calm. I wanted him to really listen to me. "You know this." I whispered.

He looked at me with a look I hadn't seen in a long time. A gentle look. Then he nodded then handed me the phone back,"Call him." He stormed off.

*****

That next week we were separating bulls to send off with each group of momma cows. All the bulls in one pin, then we herd one into a shoot and retag them with a number to match the group of momma cows he'll breed. It's a dangerous job, separating bulls but I loved it when I was younger because of that reason. Now? Not so much. But it comes with the job.

Colby and Ryan leaned on the gate next to me. I had made good friends with them the last week.

"You sure you wanna go in there?" Colby asked again.

I laughed,"I'll be alright. I fought off hadjis meaner them then for 4 years."

They shook their heads. "Alright." Ryan sighed,"You shoot 'um through and I'll tag 'em. We'll put Lloyd in there on a horse too. Seemed to calm them down last time a lot." And off they went.

I nodded. Lloyd pulled his horse out of the barn. "Good thinking being in there. Makes sense. Don't know why we haven't before." I petted his horses jaw.

The horse turned to me and nudged me. I chuckled.

"I don't know,"He cleared his throat,"Kinda dangerous to put one more big, scared animal in there with ya. But Rip thinks it works." He put his foot in the stirrup and jumped on.

I got pissed even just thinking about him,"And whatever he sees goes, huh?" I folded my arms.

"Yeah. Just about." Lloyd nodded. Then cleared his throat again. I opened the gate and let him in with the bulls. They already started getting riled up. I smiled. It felt good to be back and doing my job again.

I climbed up to the top of the gate and swung on leg over then waited until Ryan and Colby were ready with the tags.

Ryan gave me a thumbs up.

My adrenaline was pumping and I couldn't help but smile again as I jumped off the gate and into the pin with the feisty bulls. The second my feet hit the ground they scattered.

Lloyd hollered and tried cutting one off. I saw what he was doing and following. I yelled at the bulls and put my arms out wide. I was able to get between Lloyds horse and the bulls then scared him into the shoot. Lloyd laughed.

"One down, fourteen more to go." He said.

I chuckled and nodded.

"You miss this?" He asked jokingly.

I nodded again,"More than anything."

We were about half way done by 3pm. And we were all getting tired and slower.

Walker came up to the gate. "You want me in there to help? They're wearing yo' ass out." He took off his hat and then put it back on.

I did the same, but wiping sweat off my brow in between. Somehow, in 35 degree weather I was sweating. "Nah, I'm okay. Check on the old man though." I winked and gestured to Lloyd.

He chuckled.

"What'd you say?" Lloyd hollered.

"Nothing, Grandpa!" I teased. He shook his head.

We separated two more bulls. Then shit hit the fan.

The last four we're getting pissed. We had already taken too long. Colby took too long to tag and band so it's been too much time in a small pin with other bulls. Lloyd and I separated one from the rest. But he got pissed.

"Watch him!" Ryan yelled as if it weren't the only thing we were paying attention too.

The bull tried charging the horse and Lloyd.

"Get outta here!" I yelled at Lloyd, keeping my eye on the bull. He bumped against the pin.

Lloyd hesitated. He didn't wanna leave me in here alone, I understood but it was more dangerous with him.

Walker opened the gate. I felt his eyes on me. He was worried. We all were. Lloyd and his horse quickly made their way out.

I looked at the bull,"Alright boy, just me and you. Let's make this easy." I readjusted my hat again.

"You can't talk to a damn bull." I heard Walker tell Lloyd.

I walked towards the bull and hollered at him. He got startled and started towards the shoot. I followed a little but then turned around to head back to the others. He seemed under control. He was listening. But I didn't hear him running anymore. He had stopped suddenly.

"Comin' back!" Colby yelled as I turned around.

The bull had turned to me. I could see in his eyes he hated me. And there was no way he was going to be scared of me if I hollered and yelled or even whipped him. I stepped backwards towards the gate slowly.

"Im coming out." I said out loud. Ryan jumped his gate and started running to the outside of the pin to open it.

Walker shoved him away. "Don't open that. He'll push through it." Ryan stopped but not happily.

"Then how the fuck she gone get out?" He asked.

"I'm gonna jump it." I whispered. And took two steps back.

"What the fuck do you mean? You try to climb that he's gonna pin you to it!" He whisper-yelled.

I didn't answer. Just stared at the bull.

"Mary!" Ryan said again.

"Shut the fuck up, and get ready to catch my ass so I don't break anything. " I took a quick step back again. Too quick.

The bull grunted and started my way. I turned and bolted to the gate.

"Fuck!" Ryan yelled and tried to open the gate. He wouldn't have it open in time anyway. Walker was arguing with him. Yelling back and forth.

I heard the other bulls grunting and startled as well.

I jumped from the dirt ground onto the gate then took two quick steps upwards and threw myself over it as the bull hit the gate with his head with a loud clank.

Walker caught the upper half of my body but my knees and hip hit the ground hard. I felt a pop in my side and sharp pains running in my chest.

I heard other horses running as it happened. Then someone dismounting a horse. Loudly, and very pissed.

"What in the fuck is going on?!" Rip yelled and started in my direction.

"Oh here we go." I mumbled as Walker let me go. I rolled onto my ass and sat with my knees pulled up. I hung my arms on them. "Separating bulls. Where you been?" I teased sarcastically.

He pointed a finger at Walker,"Doesn't fucking look like separating to me. Why the fuck was no one in there with her?"

"No one crazy enough to." He shoved his pockets in his hands and looked up at Rip under his hat.

Rip clenched his jaw and turned around to Ryan.

"Give me an actual goddamn reason." He grumbled.

Ryan pointed up at Lloyd, still on the horse. "He was. But the horse kept pissing the bulls off."

Rip wiped his beard with his hand, trying to control his temper. Then he looked down at me on the ground.

He kneeled down and looked me in the eyes. I lifted my head up so I could see better from under my hat.

"You're gonna get yourself killed doing cowboy shit like that-" He spoke harshly.

I interrupted him,"It has to be done and we have no other help." I spat back.

"You ain't a fucking cowboy!" He raised his voice which made me jump a little,"And I aint talking about separating 'em. I'm talking 'bout jumping the gate like a fucking idiot. You should've waited until we got others in there with you. You're gonna get killed doing that shit!" He stood up and turned around.

I took a deep breath and popped up,"Ain't a cowboy, huh? I thought you said you was gonna treat me like a wrangler. Treat me like I'm just like everyone else." I called after him.

He stopped and turned around. "Barn, now." He pointed. I started to walk that way but stopped halfway.

"No, whatever you wanna say, say it here." I said calmly.

He walked up closer to me. Close to me. His eyes were full of hatred. "Get your ass to my cabin when you're done tonight. We'll fucking talk about it then." He said quietly but harshly. No one else could hear.

Normally I would speak up and asked back why not now. But it felt different. I looked up at him. I was worried. It felt like something wasn't right.

His face softened, something I rarely saw, and especially not to me recently.

"Do you understand me?" He whispered.

I nodded,"Yes sir." I swallowed hard. Then turned around walked back to Ryan.

"Ya alright?" Colby jogged up to us.

I faked a smile,"Just a little dirt."

"Come on," Walker smacked my shoulder,"Cowboy." He winked.

Ryan chuckled,"Cowboy." Then he shook his head.

$$3$$

T he whole afternoon slowed down now. I was nervous to go see Rip. Afraid of what he was going to say.

But the sun was finally setting and the work was mostly done for the day. As much as we could get done anyway. I trudged back to the house. Slowly and limping because of how sore I was. I took the steps into the house one at a time, my hip felt like it was replaced with jello and pin needles.

"Hey Mary." Kayce slapped my back on the way up the stairs.

I groaned,"Hey, Kase." I grumbled.

He chuckled,"Howd the ground feel?"

I finished the stairs and walked through the screen door. "You heard?" I asked.

"Oh yeah... Cowboy." He followed in behind me.

I turned and looked at the stairs for my bedroom and bathroom. "Fuck." I exhaled.

He laughed and walked by.

"What's funny, Kayce?" Dad said as he walked up to me. I straight my back.

"Yeah, Kase?" I asked loudly.

Dad looked down at me. "How was today?" He asked.

Fuck he knows.

I swallowed hard,"Good. Got the bulls tagged. They're going out with the mommas in the morning."

I started up the stairs as normal as possible.

"Any problems?" He asked.

I looked down the stairs at him and shook my head. "No. No problems, sir."

"Mhmm." He grumbled and walked on.

I released a deep breath and leaned against the wall. Beth was coming down the stairs.

"You look like hell." She ruffled her eyebrows.

"I know." I groaned.

*****

I took off my dirt covered clothes and tossed them into the hamper then turned to the mirror.

Bruises were forming down my entire left side, the side that took the brunt of everything. My left knee was swollen and my hip bruised. My rib cage looked awkward on the left side too. It was turning black in places. My back hurt every time I breathed in.

I stepped into the shower and did my best to wash but everything hurt so bad I made it a quick one. I slipped out of the shower and towel dried my hair. I pulled in an army sweatshirt and jeans. I pulled my Carhartt vest on over the sweatshirt and put socks and boots on. I looked in the mirror, suddenly conscious of how I looked.

I slipped out my room and downstairs. Beth sat on the couch drinking a glass of wine.

I stared down at her.

"What?" She asked.

I sighed. "Rip asked me to come to his cabin."

"And you're wearing that?" She scoffed.

I nodded and sat down next to her,"Yeah because he's pissed at me."

"But you like him?" She threw back the rest of her wine.

"Fuck no," I paused,"Well...no. I don't think so. Not yet. Like he's fucking hot. But not the personality. He's turned into an ass." I leaned forward and poured us two glasses of whiskey then gave one to her.

"Daddy, made him into an ass." She sipped the whiskey,"But, there's no way he invited you over to get mad at you. If he wanted to yell and carry on he would've done it at the barn in front of everyone. You know, male dominance." She slung the rest of her whiskey into her mouth.

I nodded,"That's what I was thinking." Then did the same with my whiskey. I poured one more glass, half way and sipped it as Beth talked. Catching me up on what happened during the governors meeting. Nothing exciting yet.

After my whiskey was gone I stood up and made my way out the door, realizing my pain wasn't as bad with the whiskey numbing it. I walked slowly to Rips cabin, oddly wanting him to wait for me. I could've drove and been there in seconds but I chose to walk through the pasture.

I could see him sitting in the front porch, the front door wide open and the porch light on.

I walked up the steps with my boots clunking.

I sat down in the rocking chair beside him. He handed me a Coors. I twisted off the top and took a long drink.

"Kayce said you're having troubles sleeping." Rip took a drink of his beer too. Talking to me in a normal voice, trying to have a normal conversation for the first time in weeks.

"Yeah. Don't know why it's any of his business." I took another drink, still salty about how he'd been acting before. But then he looked over at me. My eyes met his. And everything changed. Maybe it was the whiskey from earlier making me feel this way but he looked sincere and made me feel cared for. And comforted.

"Maybe because you woke him up hollering for back up." He said quietly.

Never mind. I looked back out at the world in front of us. A couple wolves howled but they were far away. I took another long swig of the beer. He was trying. Or at least it seemed like he was trying.

"Bravo uniform." I said, putting in a little effort myself.

"Hm?" He asked and looked back at me.
"Back up." I whispered, "Bravo uniform. That's the last thing I ever said over the radio... at least that they heard." I looked him in the eyes.

He nodded slowly,"Kayce said you weren't suppose to be home until summer. But they sent you home after everything happened instead."

I swallowed hard. "Yeah." I finished my beer. "Got another one of those?" I asked, wanting to change the subject.

"Yeah." He walked into the cabin. I heard the fridge open and bottles clink then the door close. "Here."

"Thanks." I popped off the cap and drank.

We drank in silence for a while. Then we drank more. And more.

"Alright I'm out." Rip threw his hands up coming out of the cabin.

"Out?" I laughed, the alcohol really affecting me.

"Yeah, out." He chuckled. The first laugh I had seen from him since I had been back.

I smiled up at him. Happy to see him like this. "Well damn." I rocked back and forth in the chair.

"Because you need anymore." He teased.

I smiled widely and shook my head,"You're probably right. That walk back home is gonna be rough."

A small smile danced on his face. He leaned against the door frame,"You're more than welcome to stay here. I can sleep in the bunkhouse for the night."

"Honey, if I'm staying here then you are too." I joked and drank what little was left in the glass bottle. I pulled out my pack of cigarettes and put one between my teeth.

He shook his head and leaned down to me,"Yeah you don't need those either." He grabbed the pack from my hand and the one from between my teeth.

I stood up and sat the bottle on the porch rail with a loud clink. "You seem to always know what I do and don't fucking need." My accent rang out strong, like it always does when I drink.

He folded his arms,"I always thought they'd fucking fix your smart mouth overseas, but I guess not." He said hostility. The alcohol obviously affecting him too.

I clenched my jaw. "I spent almost six years with men that thought they were better than me. I let them walk and talk over me for a couple years but that shits over."

He shook his head,"Im not trying to walk over you. Or talk above you. But goddammit I'm trying to keep you safe." His voice rose a little bit.

"Safe?" I laughed. I sighed and turned around, facing the world. "I don't know what safe is." I whispered and started to walk down the stairs. Suddenly I heard a popping and my left side had a sharp pain run through it. "Ah!" I grabbed it.

"Damn it." Rip immediately wrapped his arm around me and then lifted my legs up off the ground. He carried me inside and laid me onto a bed. He pulled my sweatshirt up. "Looks like a broken rib. I knew it the minute I saw you fall this afternoon." He placed his hand lightly on my side. I winced. Not even the alcohol was helping with the pain.

I tried to control my breathing and slow my heart rate to help with the pain. Rip was twisting ice up into a towel.

"Take off your fucking shirt." He ordered.

I looked up at him,"Yes sir." I winked, realizing at this point, I wasn't even buzzed, I was drunk.

"Goddammit, Mary. Quit fucking around, you're hurt." He put his hand behind my back to try and help me sit up. I groaned as I did. He helped me take off my sweatshirt. My vest had came off a while ago when the alcohol made me warm earlier.

I was thankful I decided to put a bra on before I left the house earlier, I almost didn't. And I had put on a sexy one. A black lacy push up.

Rip glanced at it then focused back at my ribs. He sat the ice on it and I winced again. He moved it around. And I kept wincing.

I laid there for a bit. My eyes drooping from the long day and the alcohol. The room spinning slightly.

Rip leaned over me and put his hand on my face,"Ya alright?" He whispered.

I shoved his hand away,"Fucking quit."

He looked around then back down at me.

"What? You wanna play nice now?" I questioned with an attitude.

I could see him swallow hard. He turned around and looked every where but at me. He was trying to control his temper.

"What's going on? Why do you want me here?" I spoke up. My drunkenness making my mouth say exactly what it was thinking and when.

He wiped his beard and put his fingers through his belt loops. Then he paced around.

"Are you not listening to me?" I started to get up but everything hurt so I laid back down.

He snapped around,"I'm trying to figure out how to fucking kill ya and not hurt ya." He released a deep breath.

"Do it." I whispered.

He ruffled his eyebrows. "What'd you say?"

"Do it! You think I haven't looked death in the face? Every fucking day for the past four years! You try. I'm not fucking scared." I was drunk and emotions were flying. I was saying things I would've never said sober.

He scoffed,"You've lost your fucking mind." He shook his head.

Then he chuckled. And it turned into a laugh.

"What the fuck are you laughing at?" I asked.

He kept chuckling.

I stood up, groaning and holding my side. I walked up to him and shoved him with all I could. He didn't move much.

He put his hands up. "Come on, now. Don't do this shit." He shook his head. "Lay back down, you're gonna get hurt worse."

"No." I spoke up.

He took his cowboy hat off and sat it on the kitchen table. "No?" He huffed.

"I ain't getting hurt unless you're the one doing it." I swallowed hard and straight my shoulders as much as possible.

His face softened,"I'm not gonna hurt you." He whispered.

I bit my tongue between my teeth,"Why not? You did the other day? When you grabbed my fucking mouth? Remember that?! Huh?" I shoved him hard.

"Stop." He said quietly and stepped back.

"Come on. I thought you wanted to kill me. Do it." I shoved him again. Trying to get his temper to rise.

"Fucking quit. Sit your ass down." He said a little louder.

"No, sir." I shoved again, by now we were at the wall of the house. I grunted as I did so, from pain and frustration.

He was breathing hard. We both were.

I was inches from his face. "I don't know who you are anymore but you've changed. And I fucking hate you. I hate who you've turned into." I whispered. My voice shook.

He released a breath. "Mary." He shook his head.

I grabbed my sweatshirt off the cough and pulled it on. I winced as I did. Then I started out the door. Wobbly and drunk. And down the front porch steps.

A few tears ran down my face. I wiped them away with the back of my hand.

That night I had the worst nightmares I had ever had.

Kayce kept waking me up but they started back right where they left off.

"Mary, wake up! You're home!" I heard his voice yelling. With fear. "Put down the gun. Please."

I blinked a couple times. I was holding my pistol. Pointing it at my bedroom window. Kayce was behind me.

"Are you awake?" He whispered.

I breathed hard,"I think so." I whispered back.

He put a hand on my shoulder.

I flipped the safety on my pistol and handed it to him. He grabbed it and put it in his jeans behind his back.

"Come here." He pulled me into a hug again. For the third time that night. Or morning I should say. "You gotta stay calm during the day. You go to sleep mad or hurting or upset, it's gonna make them worse." He rubbed my back. I didn't have the heart to tell him it hurt.

Those are my only three emotions. I thought to myself.

4

The next day I slowly got up and got changed. It was a Saturday. So maybe half the amount of work needed to be done.

I trudged my way to the barn, trying to keep up with Kayce but my side hurt so bad I could hardly stand it.

I saddled my horse but it took me forever. Then I tried to get on it. "Ah. Ah." I groaned and breathed hard.

"Ya alright, cowboy?" Walker hollered to me.

"Uhhh," I tried again and made it this time. "I'm alright."

"Mhmm." He rode past me.

Gonna be a long day.

*****

"What the hell are you doing on a horse?" Llyod asked me.

"Gonna move some cows." I said like a smart ass.

"Get off that damn thing, you've got a broken rib. And who knows what else." He ordered as he rode past me. "I'll take your spot." I opened my mouth to argue,"This ain't an option, Mary. Get your ass home and get some rest so you can be ready on Monday." He pointed back to the barn.

I sighed but he was right. And I was hurting.

I slowly rode back to the barn. But I could see trouble riding straight to me.

Rip rode up to me,"What in the fuck is wrong with you?"

I didn't say a word to him. My horse walked past him. I stopped my horse, about to tell him something. That I didn't mean what I said last night, or I shouldn't of tried to piss him off so bad. But I continued riding.

One day in bed turned to three. I could barely move.

Dad came in. "You haven't been to the barn in three days. You must really be hurting." He sat on the side of my bed.

I nodded. "I'll be good in another day or two. Just trying to healing it so it doesn't get worse."

He nodded. Then he patted my leg on top of the covers. "Smart girl. Holler if you need something. Beth and I are going to Helena for a few days. Work to be done." He kissed my forehead then walked out.

Kayce was there for a while that night. We sat in the living room and drank beer and whiskey and talked about the military and our childhood. We drank too much but he decided he wanted to go the bar with some of the wranglers. I didn't feel like it yet.

So it was just me in an empty house. Soon I fell asleep and kept having the nightmares. Even worse this time.

And I kept hearing noises when I would wake up from them. People walking up the stairs. Radio codes going off. Helicopters constantly. And I was nearly paralyzed. I didn't feel safe and I was getting overwhelmed.

I needed someone.

I grabbed my phone, tears streaming done my face and called Kayce. But he didn't answer. I called Beth, no answer. I called Llyod, no answer. And Walker and Ryan and Colby. No answer.

I looked at Rips name. My hands were shaking.

Bravo uniform. I could hear Jake screaming. Bravo uniform. Bird. Send a bird. Now. Bravo uniform. Then gunfire.

I jumped and clicked on Rips name.

"Hello?" He answered in one ring.

"Rip." I started to cry. I needed him. I needed someone to protect me.

"I'm coming, Mary. What's going on?" He sounded calm but I could hear him running.

I heard more gunfire and screaming. I could smell burning flesh.

"Bravo..." I swallowed hard. He won't know. "I need you. They're everywhere." I cried. Tears streamed down my face.

"I'll be there in a minute. I promise. Hang in there-"

Then nothing. Radio silence.

I closed my eyes hard. And tried to wish it all away. Trying to to decipher what was real and not real. Twenty minutes passed maybe. I couldn't tell. Then I heard the front door slam. And seconds later I felt hands on my face.

"No! No! Stop!" I screamed and reached for a knife that wasn't on leg but was suppose to be.

"Mary, open your eyes. It's me." Rip put his thumbs on my eye lids and pulled up gently. "It's me." He whispered. And all the noises stopped.

I focused in on him. Black hair and black beard. Dark brown eyes that looked safe. I reached up touched his face with my finger tips. They brushed across his scruffy beard.

"Rip?" I whispered. He sat down in the side of my bed. He proper himself up with one arm on one side me.

He gave a small smile,"Yeah. It's Rip. Im here, darling. You're okay, now." I dropped my hands. He pushed my hair off my forehead and out of my face.

I released a breath I didn't know I was holding. "I'm safe?" I whispered.

"If I'm here, you're always safe. I promise." His voice was raspy. He had either been asleep, or he was at the bar, smoking and drinking. Probably at the bar with Kasey.

I took a deep breath and smelled the familiar Marlboro Red smoke. "I thought you quit smoking." I asked in a small voice. Realizing I was still drunk.

He chuckled,"I tried." He must be a little drunk too.

I stared up at his eyes, comparing them to how kind they looked right now versus the other night at the cabin.

"This is the Rip I remember." I whispered.

He nodded. "I know. A lot happened while you were gone." He cleared his throat.

"I didn't mean what I did the other night. I don't hate you-" A tear ran down my face.

"Hey now," He brushed my tears away quickly,"let's not talk about that."

"I thought about you a lot when I was gone. And then I came home and you're someone else." Drunk me said without even thinking.

He just stared down at me. "I-I don't know."

"I don't know why they think they can just send us all home. After everything we saw. They just expect us to be strong enough. And some guys are. But I'm not." I shook my head.

"You're strong, Mary. The strongest person I know." He sweetly.

I exhaled deeply then sat up. I was feeling better. I stared at him. He grew up to be a very attractive man. Between the beard and the broad shoulders and stout arms, he was nearly perfect. And he smelled of beer and cigarettes, the best cologne a man could wear in my opinion. I was just noticing how much I liked how this man looked. If I was at the bar, he would've been the man I flirted with. I would've bet him a game of pool and most definitely whooped his ass. Then I'd tell him that loser buys the drinks and have him buy us a few until I was giggly and looking at him with longing eyes. Then I'd let him take me home. We'd hook up and I'd never see him again.

"Can we go to your cabin?" I asked. "I wanna start the other night over."

He smiled and gave me an answer that made chills form on my body,"Come on, girl." He moved my covers back. My bare legs were exposed. A large scar ran down my thigh all the way to my shin. He stared at it. Then looked at me.

"Fucking hadjis." I shook my head and stood up slowly. "Once they got Jake and I that night, they drug us to their station. Literally drug us,"I dropped my shorts and pulled on a pair of jeans,"My leg got caught on a rock. And they kept pulling. Tore it right open. Bout bled to death if it wouldn't have been packed with dirt and shit." I didn't mind to talk about my army days when I was drunk. I liked how people acted when I tell them the crazy shit we all went through.

I pulled my shirt off then walked to my closet.

"For fucks sake Mary." Rip looked down at the ground.

I stopped and smiled then turned back around to face him. "You can look. I don't mind." My chest was exposed as I held the sweatshirt in my hand.

"I think your daddy might." He chuckled, stilling looking down, his hat shielding his face.

"Say that again."I whispered,"I like when you say that."

"Goddamn it." He shook his head and walked out my door.

I laughed and pulled the sweatshirt on. Then slipped on socks and a vest.

I walked down the stairs. Rip was in the kitchen, his hands flat on the counter leaning forward. He was breathing hard.

I took a swig out of the whiskey beside the staircase. And another. Then walked into the kitchen.

"Ya alright?" I asked getting close to him and putting my hand on his back for two reasons. One because I just wanted to touch him. I wanted to run my hands around his arms and across his firm shoulders then hold his face in my hands and feel his scruffy beard. Two because I was wobbly on my feet from the alcohol.

He released a deep breath,"I don't think I want you coming to the cabin." He said.

"What?" I furrowed my eyebrows and dropped my hand.

He shook his head and shoved his hands in his pockets,"Its a bad idea. You know exactly where it's gonna lead."

"Well yeah. You don't want that?" I questioned.

"Not when you're drunk. I don't want you to regret it." He started to walk out the door.

"Wait!" I grabbed his arm. He looked at my hand on his arm. I dropped it immediately. "Can you stay here?"

"Mary-" He sounded harsh.

"No, not like that. I- I just don't wanna be alone. I can't. I can't handle it. I get flashbacks and nightmares and I don't feel safe."I whispered and carried on."I'm sorry."

"Don't be sorry." He reached out to me but then stopped. "I'll stay on the couch. But go ahead and get back upstairs. You need rest."

I bit my tongue. Then nodded. "Yes, sir." I started walking up the stairs.

"Mary," He called after me. I turned and looked down at him,"Stop calling me sir." He shook his head then started to smirk.

He was back to the Rip I was with just moments earlier.

"Does it bother you?" I winked and grinned.

He nodded a little,"Only when you say it. Now get your little ass up there before you get me in trouble."

"Yes, sir." I smiled and ran up the stairs.

I heard him cursing.

5

My body self healed within a week but I was back in the saddle by day five. I couldn't stand it any longer.

Winter was right around the corner so there was a lot of work to be done, what dad had referred to when I first got home.

The biggest was bailing hay. Most of which was already done. The next was vaccines. None of which had been done.

Walker and Ryan roped the calves and Llyod helped me hold them down while I shot the vaccines into the little guys. Jimmy leaned against the fence, just watching how things worked.

"So you can't rope?" I hollered at him.

"Uh no. I don't know how." He stuttered.

"What kinda cowboy is he?" I chuckled and shoved the needle into the steer then injection the liquid into him.

"He's a rescue." Walker rode up next to me, "Didn't even know how to ride a fucking horse at first."

I nodded,"Damn. I'm surprised. He can break a horse like nobody's business." I wiped the swipe off my upper lip.

"He use to be a bull rider." Lloyd grumbled as he took the next steer to the ground.

"Ah. I see." I injected the next steer.

"Mary Margaret!"

I jumped as I heard my full name yelled. Dad was yelling it. But where the fuck was he?

I looked around carefully.

"He's over there." Lloyd said quietly and took the shots from me while pointing towards the barn. "You want me to come with?" He whispered.

I stared at my father, stomping towards us. He was pissed.

"Uh," I chewed on my bottom lip,"I think I'm okay. I haven't done anything yet."

Except hit on Rip. But Rip wouldn't have said anything.

I walked to the edge of the pen then climbed over the gate as dad was approaching it.

"Yes sir?" I asked rubbing my hands together to brush the dirt off.

He clenched his jaw,"We have a problem." He looked around then shoved his hands in his pockets.

"What's going on?" I readjusted my hat.

He lowered his voice,"We've got people snooping around down by pasture 9. Caught 'em on the cameras."

Cameras? When the fuck did we get cameras? I put my hands in my pockets just like he did. A habit I made myself do when I was a kid, so I could look and act like him. Now it was natural.

"There was some fence cut down there the other day. What do you think they want?" I asked.

"I don't know. But I want you to take a camp down there and stay for a couple nights. Maybe scare um away." He started to walk away.

"Yes sir. I'll see who Rip wants to keep here to work first-"

"Don't ask him. He's not your boss, Mary. You have the name. This is your ranch. You take who you need and he can do his job around you." He raised his voice a little.

I swallowed hard.

"Do you understand? You're not a wrangler. You don't work for him. He works for us. And you tell him that." Dad had a look in his eyes. Something had happened that he wasn't telling me.

"Yes sir." I nodded. "I don't work for him."

He looked out at the world around us, watching Jimmy badly rope. "Mary, you never know if there's gonna be a time where you have to run this ranch. You need everyone to respect you and listen to you. You're a Dutton. This is your ranch. You don't work for it, you own it, dammit. Start acting like it." He mumbled and started to walk away. Then he stopped, "The wranglers treat you like a wrangler. Not like a Dutton. And if you don't start acting like a Dutton, I'll put you in the bunkhouse like a wrangler. You take your pick. Got it?"

I nodded nervously.

"Good. Be careful." He dropped his head and started to walk off.

I kicked the dirt around with my boots, cussing myself. Rip and I were finally not trying to kill each other and my father had to throw this into the mess. All I wanna do is work. Just help the cattle and that's all. I just wanna be a wrangler.

*****

We finished up work that day and I followed everyone into the bunk house like I normally would. I tried to think hard about who Rip would need tonight and in the morning. But I drew a blank.

"Dad wants us to set up a camp on pasture 9. Says there's someone sneaking around down there. Colby, Jimmy, and Clint, pack your shit. Going camping boys." I grabbed a beer out of the fridge and took a long drink.

"Rip wanted me to load the mules in the morning. They're going to that training camp. So I'm out." Clint chuckled.

I nodded, and started to ask Ryan. But I heard my dad in the back of my head. This is your ranch. Rip works for us.

"And?" I said out loud.

Clint sat down at the dinner table and looked up at me,"I already got shit to do, tomorrow. I ain't gonna waste my time camping."

Lloyd stood up,"Just do what she fucking says. No reason to be talking back." Dad must've talked to Lloyd.

I kicked myself internally. If Lloyd knows then I'll have to play it on in case dad gets him anything.

Clint shook his head,"Why? Cause she's a damn woman?"

Here we go. I swallowed hard, not want to say what I was about to say.

"Cause it's my fucking ranch." I spoke loud and clear. Everyone looked over at me. Most nodded with approval. They all respected me and I had never had a problem until now. "We leave in an hour." I started for the door.

"It's your daddy's ranch." Clint said.

I stopped and spun on my heals. My blood boiled. Then walked up to him. I stood between his legs and leaned down to his face.

"It may be my daddy's ranch but it doesn't run without me. Or Kayce. Or Beth. Or fucking Jamie. It would've been in the ground if wasn't for Lee. So you listen here," I sat down and straddled his lap. He leaned back as far as possible and moved around. He put his hands on the chair, trying to find a place for them to go. "It's my fucking ranch too. You may work for Rip. But Rip works for my daddy. You should really just do as you're told-" I leaned in closer to making him uncomfortable but the door slung open.

"What the fuck is fucking going on?!" Rip kicked the trash can by the door and it flew halfway across the room. Everyone jumped but no one had an answer.

"Great timing." I whispered to Clint. I rested my extended arm on his shoulder and looked back at Rip. His face was bright red and his fist were clenched. "Just talking about going camping with my new best friend here." I patted Clints chest. He swallowed hard, eyes wide.

"Camping, huh? Don't look like camping." He huffed.

"It will later." I winked at Clint and stood up slowly. "Anyway," I stretched the word out. "Colby, Jimmy, Clint and I are camping in pasture nine tonight because of what was on the cameras. Clint said he had other shit to do tomorrow. We were trying to work out the kinks." I took another drink out of my beer.

Rip drew her anger from me to Clint,"When she tells you to do something you do it. She may be a pain the ass but she still owns this place. You hear me?"

"Yes sir." He nodded.

"Mary. A word?" Rip started out the door.

"Yeah," I grabbed myself another beer and one for Rip,"An hour." I winked at Clint.

6

Rip was leaned against the corral panels. I cracked open a beer and handed it to him.

"Thanks, babe." He took it and tipped it back.

"Babe?" I chuckled. "Man, that yes sir thing really does work on you."

He was breathing hard.

"Are you okay?" I asked.

He shook his head. "No." He took another long drink then tossed the empty can. "I bout fucking killed him in there." He looked me in the eyes. "Seeing you on his lap." He turned around and gripped the panel tightly. It looked as if it would crumble in his hands.

"Well for fucks sake, Rip." I started to storm away.

"How about next time you ask me before you take a bunch of boys camping?" He spoke up.

Here came the dreaded words I didn't wanna say.

"Because its my-" I couldn't say it. There's no way. "Because dad said not to." Is what came out.

He stared at me. "Cause I work for you?" He said hatefully.

"I didn't say that, Rip." I walked back to him.

"No," He shook his head,"That's what he told you. He talked to me about it. And it's true-"

"Im not like him. You don't work for me. The wranglers work for you. You work for my father. I just happened to have the last name."

He reached out and put his hand on my shoulder,"Next time fucking tell me. I could've talked to Clint. You don't have to scare the hell out of him."

I brushed his hand off hatefully. "I don't need you to do my work. He just forgot where I came from. He respects me now." I released a deep breath and looked out at the bright moon in the sky. "Rip?" I asked quietly. He looked down at me. I rested my hand on his chest.

He stepped to the side,"Stop."

I took a step back and shook my head. "Where do I stand with you?"

He opened his mouth to speak then closed it. He didn't have an answer.

"I need to know. Because one minute you're mad at me. You act like you fucking hate me. And within seconds you're inviting me to the cabin and calling me babe." I felt a lump in my throat form but I pushed it down. "I don't give a fuck which was it is. I rather you hate me to be honest. Because at this point it would be easier. But pick a side, goddamn it. Because I don't know whether to let myself fall in love with you or keep hating you." A tear slipped from my eye. I quickly brushed it away. "Make up your fucking mind and let me know." I stormed away to the house to grab my camping gear.

*****

We rode out to pasture nine. It was a good 3,000 acres out from the bunk house. We were setting up camp in the dark just right on the other side of the fence, not even twenty feet away.

Dad said there were people but never how many so we packed plenty of ammunition just in case.

"You wanna do shifts in twos? It's a lotta ground out here." I asked Jimmy while nailing the tent into the ground.

"Y-you're asking me?" He stuttered.

I chuckled,"No I'm talking to this nail I'mma beating on. Yes dammit, asking you. Whatcha think we should do?" I stood up straight with my hands on my hips.

He readjusted his hat,"Uh, honestly? I think one all night and one switch-ing off would be fine. It's quiet out here and you can hear anything. Switch after 3 hours. That puts us at daylight."

I nodded,"Good plan. You done this before?"

He nodded too,"Yes ma'am. A couple times."

I threw my sleeping bag in the tent, knowing I didn't plan on using it. "Don't call me ma'am, Jimmy. I'm probably younger then you." I chuck-led.

"I'm 26." He laughed.

"Yeah. Almost 25."

"So you did two tours in Afghanistan?" Jimmy started a fire after the other two laid down the wood.

I grabbed a bottle of whiskey from my saddle bag. "A tour in Korea. A tour and a half in Afghanistan." I grabbed my thermos and filled it about half way then screw the lid on.

"I bet you're glad you got outta there early. I heard about everything that happened out there on the news." He sat down and leaned against a log.

Colby shook his head then took off his hat and ran a hand through his hair. "Jimmy..." he sighed and looked up at the sky.

Jimmy looked over at him confused,"What? You didn't hear about that? There snipers that were kidnapped and then the embassy was taken over and the president pulled everyone out. That shit was terrible."

"Jimmy." Colby said it again harsher.

I chuckled,"It's okay." I nodded to Colby. "Yeah, it was bad, Jimmy. But you're wrong," I took a sip of the whiskey, it warm my chest all the way down,"They didn't completely take over the embassy. We held it down until more troops arrived. 107 hours later." I sat down on the log beside him.

He stared up at me,"You were there?"

I gave a small smile, proud of my team and myself and what we had done. "Yes sir. From start to finish."

"Wow." He looked at the fire. We were all quiet.

"I don't think any of us has ever told you to your face, but we're proud of you, Cowboy. And thank you for everything you did for our country." Clint grabbed my shoulder and squeezed.

I nodded, not knowing what to say. I never knew how to answer so I just never did.

"What shift do you want, Cowboy?" Colby asked before going to bed. "The all night?"

"Yeah-" I stood up and dusted off my ass, knowing the amount of dirt on it.

"No, I'll get it." Jimmy stepped in.

I chuckled,"Jimmy, my job was staying up for days in end. Lemme do what I'm good at."

He froze. "You were one of the snipers." He said quietly. My smile fell. I nodded a little. "I didn't know. I'm sorry." His voice trailed off.

"It's okay." I whispered and patted his chest. "I'm alive. That's all that matters." I refilled my whiskey glass. "Clint, you better sleep first so you'll be ready to load mules tomorrow. You'll have to leave here by four to get there in time." I winked at him.

He shook his head and went into his tent.

7

I loved camping. It was the one thing we use to all do as a family. Go camping, go fishing, come back to camp and cook the fish. Then mom would make biscuits and Kayce would eat most of them. The five of us kids would all sleep in one tent. But we barely ever slept. Usually just told each other ghost stories until we were so scared we couldn't sleep. Then the next day we would lay out in the pastures on a quilt and take a nap.

Maybe it was the open sky and cool wind but warm sun. And all the nature noises. Whether it's crickets or wolves or owls. They were all familiar to me.

That's why an unfamiliar sound made my bones run cold. Walking. A human walking. Then a horse walking. The ground crunching under someone's feet.

I glanced over at Colby. He was leaned against the log, asleep. He had fell asleep about ten minutes ago and I let him. The man was tired.

I grabbed my M16 and put it to my shoulder while standing up just enough to be crouching. I quietly walked towards the tree line I heard the walking from. Whoever it was didn't know we were here or didn't care. They were a loud walker.

I held my flashlight under my gun and wait until they got closer.

My heart started to race and my adrenaline rushed cold through me.

I could them almost close them.

Only a few more feet.

I turned from behind a tree and flicked my flashlight on, finger tight on the trigger.

I was meet with a cowboy in a black coat.

"Goddammit, Rip." I flipped off the light and aimed my gun down. "I almost shot you."

"I noticed." He nodded,"Theres another problem. Let's get back to your camp." He whispered and put his hand on my back, hurrying me forward. "We gotta get you outta here. Everyone. Pack up everything. Now!" He said when we made it back. He kicked Colby awake and opened the boys tents. He helped me pulled up the tents.

"Why? What's going on?" Jimmy asked nervously.

I started to pack everything into my saddle bag.

"There was a helicopter circling the other pastures," He grabbed the cooler and dumped it on the fire, putting out the flames,"They already tried to drop a fire bomb down but it didn't go off. Dropped a couple people off in another pasture, heading this way. Not sure what's going but they'll be here soon." Rip helped Jimmy with his tent.

I froze. "Helicopter?" I whispered.

Rip stopped and looked up at me. He walked up to me,"You okay?."

"Rip, I-I don't know. I don't know if I can handle it. Just the noises, it'll-." I whispered, afraid the others would hear me. Rip stopped me. He understood.

So he nodded and tossed a bag straight into Jimmys gut. Jimmy caught it against his stomach and groaned slightly. "You guys go. We'll pack up and head out. I want as much help on the other pastures in case they come back."

They all listened and dropped everything then jumped on their horses and took off quick.

I helped Rip pack as quick as I could, involuntarily listening for the deafening noise of the propellers in the air. But they hadn't came yet. I also tried to listen for foot steps that weren't ours but didn't hear any of that either.

We grabbed all the gear and packed it on our two horses, which meant we were gonna be moving even slower now.

We were within 800 acres of the bunkhouse when I heard a familiar thumping.

My stomach flipped. Stay with it Mary. Ignore it.

I saw Rip glance over at me. But I didn't look back. I kept on.

The thumping got louder and louder. I could feel it in my chest. Fight it.

Then I started to hear faint screams and gunfire. Then everything got blurry. My horse kept running. But I was wanting to stop.

"Stop." I dropped the reins. "Stop!" I yelled. My horse stopped almost on a dime, although this wasn't how he was trained with to stop. He just knew.

I jumped off the horse and landed on my stomach onto the ground. My hands flew behind my head.

I scrambled. Where's my helmet?

"Mary, come on! We gotta go!" I heard someone yelling, and felt their hand on my back.

"Get down, private!" I yelled back. The thumping got louder. They're gonna see us on the ground. I laid down as flat as possible and covered my head. "You're gonna get us blown to bits!" I covered my ears, the thumping getting so loud it hurt my head.

"Come on, Mary. We gotta get to the other pastures. They need the help." He spoke loudly over the helicopters deafening noise.

I tensed every muscle in my body, waiting for the shaking of the ground from the bombs or the loud shots of bullets being thrown around us. They had to have seen us.

"I'm sorry, Mary." I heard someone whispered then pick me up from the ground.

I fought and screamed and kicked and punched. I made contact but still I felt myself being carried.

"No! Nooo!" I covered my ears and screamed. I went almost completely limp in fear and shock. I squeezed my eyes closed and kept my ears covered. I leaned completely into the persons chest for protection. Their body would block most of the shrapnel. I said I'd never be taken hostage again. But I couldn't fight. My body was nearly paralyzed. Maybe I had been hit.

What felt like hours later we stopped and I was drug down from a horse. I fought more until I was carried somewhere. I was put down and I collapsed onto the floor.

"Mary! Mary look at me!" Someone keep saying loudly. I shuffled my back against a wall. Screaming still.

It was forever of me covering my ears and keeping my ears closed. The only way to protect myself from the outside.

"Corporal, they're sending in a dust off for wounded. You wanna give the orders?" I heard a different voice talking.

I calmed a little and thought hard. This is a fellow soldier. He's safe.

I gave coordinates to my last known locations. At the camp. Camp. What camp? Why was I at a camp?

"All clear, Corporal." It said.

I released a deep breath and slowly opened my eyes. Kayce was crouched in front of me. And I was in Rips cabin.

"What happened?" I whispered, extremely embarrassed. I wanted to curl up in my bed and never wake up.

"Helicopter caused a flashback." He whispered back.

I looked around him. Rip was standing at the door.

"Did anyone else see?" I asked.

"No," he glanced back at Rip,"He made sure they were ahead of you. And he brought you to his cabin so they wouldn't see anything at all. I was hoping you wouldn't freak out and not know where you were. I know you've never been here before." He stood up and looked around. "You've done a lot of work on the place. It looks good." He acted as if what had happened was normal. For him, it probably was.

"Yeah, thanks." Rip nodded and wiped his lip, blood dripping from it.

Kayce also doesn't know I was here before.

Kayce sat me with for a long while with he arms wrapped around my shoulders.

"If you're okay, I'm gonna go check on the pastures again. Give someone a break." He patted my head and walked out.

I looked around slowly then stood up.

"Do you need anything?" Rip asked. He was clearing uncomfortable and I didn't blame him.

"Sleep." I teased.

"Then get some sleep. If you need anything call me, okay?" He started to walk out.

"Wait!" I stopped him. He turned around with worried eyes,"You don't have to stay in the bunkhouse." I whispered.

He nodded,"Okay. I'm gonna check pastures and then I'll be back." And he was gone. I wanted to go and help. But my body was exhausted. And after the flashback I had, I would be useless.

I looked around his cabin. The table and chairs were pushed around and his couch was partially moved. I'm sure it was from me. But I couldn't remember anything except for starting to ride home.

I adjusted the furniture back to normal. Then I drank a glass of water. I pulled off some of my layers from camping. I kicked off my boots and took off my jeans but left my socks. His floor was cold. I slipped off my last shirt and folded it neatly and put it with the rest of the clothes. Then I pulled a tshirt out of his dryer so I knew it was clean and put it on. It fell just above my knees and was three sizes too big. But it smelled like him and that's all I needed.

I pulled back the covers in his bed and slipped in. The sheets were cold but also like the T-shirt, smelled just like him.

I let myself sink into the comfy bed. Much more comfortable than mine.

My breathing slowed and I shut my eyes. I felt okay.

An hour or so later, the door opened quietly. My eyes were closed and I left them that way. I heard Rips boots come off. Then I felt him come closer. I heard him sigh loudly then walk away. When I heard the shower turn on I opened my eyes. I didn't know if I wanted him to stay awake and talk with me or if I wanted to act like I was still asleep then wake up tomorrow and act like none of this ever happened.

There was no telling what I said or how I acted during the flash back.

I was in deep thought when the shower turned off. Soon Rip walked out in flannel pants and a white tshirt. The strong smell of his soap filled the air. It smelled great.

"I was afraid I'd wake up." He said walking up to me.

"It's okay. I rather you wake me then smell nasty." I teased and rolled over.

He chuckled. A real smile was on his face. After everything I put him through today, he smiled at me then said, "Good night, Mary."

This was a different side of Rip. One that smiled lovingly at me and told me goodnight.

He flipped off the light switch then laid down on the couch.

I laid awake for quite some time. I never heard him snoring. I use to hear him snore when I went on late night rides with my friends and he slept in the barn.

I slowly started to drift out. But kept hearing noises that I knew weren't there. Gun fire and radio calls. I opened my eyes again and they went away. But soon my eyes were heavy and it started again.

"We can't get to you, Corporal. Not yet. We're trying." I heard a man on the other end of the extremely staticky radio.

They've made it on once, what's so different this time?

"They're gonna make it in. We can't hold them off any longer!" I yelled into it. "Send a bird again or the rest of us are all dead."

".... Sending ...at .... Hours." Was all that came through.

"No copy! ! I repeat, did not copy!"

No answer.

Jake groaned next to me,"Are they sending help?" He held his head, blood pouring out of everywhere.

I swallowed hard. He should've went the first time. I should've made him go. Now look at the mess we're in. No help on the ground and no air support.

My dry mouth hung up,"I don't know. I lost them." Jake dropped his head down,"Hey, stay with me. You gotta get through this with me!" I shook his face and he perked back up.

One of the few soldiers I had left ran into the room we were in,"Corporal, they've made it through!"

"Hey..." I heard Rips voice. My eyes shot open. He was sitting on the edge of the bed. "You okay?" He asked.

I nodded,"Yeah, sorry if I woke you up." I sat up and rubbed my face.

"You didn't. I was already awake. Heard you breathing hard, figured I'd wake you up before it got worse." He started to stand up, he grunted and held his side.

"Why don't you sleep here? That couch is probably killing you." My words trailed off quietly.

He shook his head and started to lay on the couch ,"Nah, it's ok-"

"Please." He stopped. "I just need to see someone. To realize what's real and not real." I sounded like a crazy person but it was how I felt.

"Okay." He nodded and walked over to the bed. He lifted the covers, letting cold air in and laid down beside me. He laid flat on his back with his hands folded on his chest. His face was lit up by the fire in the fireplace and he slowly closed his eyes.

I rolled onto my side and faced him. Just staring at him until I slowly drifted asleep.

And for the first time since I had been out Afghanistan, I didn't have a nightmare. I didn't even dream. I just rested.

8

I woke up the next morning. Rip wasn't beside me but I felt peaceful. Comfortable. So I just laid there. My body was completely exhausted and I was scared to see and know what happened last night.

Only a few minutes of soaking in the peace and quiet, the door opened. My dad slipped in quietly. Fuck.

"Hey." He walked up to me and sat on the edge of the bad. "Kayce told me what happened." He placed his hand on my forehead and petted the top of my head.

"Yeah." Was all I could say.

"When he came home, it was months before he could sleep again." He nodded. "How did you sleep last night?"

I sighed,"Honestly Dad, really good. I feel safe here."

He cleared his throat,"I figured so. Rip has always taken care of you when you needed anything. It's his job to make you feel safe."

"Dad..." I shook my head.

He stood up slowly. "That's why he's here, Mary. He works for us. We already talked about this-"

"You talked, I listened." I sassed.

He huffed,"Apparently not very well." He paced around for a minute, just like Rip does when he's pissed,"As soon as you get it through your thick skull that he's a wrangler, who works for us, who we pay to be here and live here and keep us safe, it'll make life a little easier." He was harsh and stern. I didn't know where this attitude about Rip was coming from. Before I left, he treated Rip like a son. Better than any of his own kids. But once again, something had happened that I wasn't told about. "And if you want to take a break from wrangling for a while, I think that's probably a good idea." He started for the door.

I sat up."Dad, I'm fine-"

I heard his boot clump across the floor back to me. "Mary, it wasn't a question. Take a break. You just got back from hell... and you need to get your shit together." And he was gone before I could say anything else.

I got up and showered. Then I pulled clothes out of my camping bag. I put on my jeans, a thermal shirt, a quarter zip sweatshirt and a vest.

I stepped outside, no shoes just socks and I sat on the porch in one of the rocking chairs. It was cold outside but I didn't care. Anything to just enjoy the fresh air. I pulled one knee up to chest then left the other one dangling to rock myself. I sat there for a long time, just watching the mountains and the trees and the critters. Soon I saw Rip walking up the hill. He was looking down but he glanced up he saw me. A small smile played on his lips.

I smiled too.

He walked up on the porch and sat next to me. "Morning."

"Hey." I nodded. "Get mules taken off?" I asked.

"Yeah, bout two hours late though." He chuckled.

Then we were quiet. I didn't mind the quiet.

"Your father talked to me and uh-" he rubbed his hands together, clearing nervous and unsure.

"He talked to me too." I nodded and he nodded with him,"He wants me to take a break from wrangling." I huffed.

Rip stood up then knelt down in front of me. I put both feet down and leaned forward on my elbow. "Mary," his voice was low and raspy,"You went through everyone's worst nightmare. Everyone in this country was terrified for y'all, but you were there." He put his hand on my leg. It felt warm and kind and caused a tight feeling in my chest. "You took care of everyone else. Now you gotta take care of yourself. That's your job right now. Pick up the pieces that are left of you, because I know most of you is gone," His voice cracked and he cleared his throat. Tears whelmed in my eyes when he said it. Because he was right and I just hadn't realized it. "Pick up what's left and try to find peace with it. Because I can't keep watching you do this to yourself." His eyes were glossy and kind.

I stared at him and thought hard. He was right. I was still living as of everyone around me wanted to kill me. I was only at peace when I was alone. Or with Rip. Then I thought About what my dad said. But I couldn't look at Rip as an employee or wrangler. Then I decided it was best to stop thinking.

I threw my arms around his neck and held tightly. Like when I first came home and everything seemed okay. It took him by surprise and knocked him backwards onto his ass. I fell with him but didn't let go. His back hit against the porch railing and knocked his hat off. I sat between his legs with my arms slung around his neck still. One of his legs were propped up and my legs fell in under it. He grabbed my waist and held me tight. Then moved one hand to the back of my head as I buried it into his neck.

"I don't know where to start." I whispered through tears.

He moved his hand from the back of my head to the side of my face. "It'll be okay. I'm not gonna let you do this alone."

I wanted to leaned in and press my lips to his so bad. I wanted to make out here on the porch where anyone could see and not care. But I heard footsteps and was frightened so I jumped up and sat back onto the chair. Rip stood up quickly and brushed himself off.

Llyod turned the corner of the cabin,"Rip, we got a problem."

9

Rip left in a hurry back down to the barn. Then I watched him and Lloyd ride off quick into the woods.

I made my way down to the barn. Jimmy was coming in on a horse. He jumped off and walked him into the barn.

I started walking his way but the smell of smoke overwhelmed my nose. Jimmy had black soot on his cheeks and his light grey hat had multiple dark spots on it too.

"Jimmy, what's going on?" I asked quietly.

He coughed and lead his horse into the stall,"Rip didn't tell you?" He coughed more and more then spit whatever came up into the ground.

"No. He didn't." I reached into the fridge in the corner of the barn and pulled out an orange Gatorade then tossed it to him.

He caught it with a loud snap,"Thanks." He twisted the cap and gulped down the liquid quickly. I watched and waited for him to finish so he could tell me what had happened. He sighed loudly and wiped his mouth with the back of his hand. "Well you know someone dropped fire down, you were there last night. It covered pasture 7 and part of 8. All the fence from

6-11 is ripped out of the ground and mangled." He paused and let out a deep breath.

"Go on." I nodded. There was more.

He took another long drink, "They killed every cow in pasture 9."

My mouth hung open. That was nearly 300 cattle. "H-how?" Probably alfalfa.

He shrugged, "Don't know yet. Half of 'em are burned up now." He looked at his boots then back up at me, "It's a mess out there, man. I've never seen anything like it." He shook his head.

I released a deep breath. "Because this is exactly what my father needs to worry about now." I kicked a five gallon bucket that was laying around, "Goddamnit." I cursed. "Who the fuck would do this to us?" I mumbled.

"Probably the people that wanna build that casino and airport." Jimmy started to unsaddle his horse. The sounds of the buckles and straps echoed in the unusually quiet barn.

"Who wants to build what?" I snapped around back to him.

He pulled the saddle off the horse and tossed it onto a saddle rack. "Some Indian wants a casino and hotel on the reservation."

My jaw dropped. I stared at him. "You're fucking kidding me?"

"Uh, no. No I'm not. No ones told you?" He coughed up some more congestion.

"Obviously fucking not." I rolled my eyes at the stupid question.

"Huh." He nodded. "I guess I probably shouldn't have been... the one to do it." He put his tongue between the ride side of his mouth. I could tell he was regretting and thinking of every word he said.

But the way he said it made me chuckle.

"It's okay. I won't tell anybody you were the one who told me." I gave him a small smile.

He gave me a look I hadn't seen from him before. It was a caring look. Like he had finally listened to the words I was saying and he believed them. For the first time, I felt like I was getting a real emotion out if Jimmy. I just didn't know which emotion it was.

"Thank you, Mary." He tossed the Gatorade bottle into the metal trash bin. "I'm gonna shower. I feel like haven't taken one in forever. And I smell like smoke. So bad." He chuckled and started to walk off.

"Jimmy?" I called after him. He turned around. "Rub an orange peel on your face, it helps with the smoke smell. And get some rest." I nodded at him. He nodded back.

"You had to deal with that a lot over seas?" He asked.

I nodded. "Yeah, I did. Lotta fires, not a lot of good soap to get the smell out. Oranges were easy to get though."

He started coughing again,"Thanks."-

It wasn't the smell of the smoke I wanted out. It was the smell of what was in the smoke. Bodies.

I saddled up a horse and started out for a long ride.

*****

I could see the smoke from miles away and started to smell it shortly after. As I rode closer I could smell the cattle that had burnt up. The smell of burned flesh made my stomach flip and my vision foggy.

"Whoa." I pulled back the reins on my horse. I took a deep breath and looked out at the mountains. The beauty all around me. And I breathed slowly, trying to keep myself here and not let my mind wonder back to Afghanistan. "Pick up what's left." I mumbled and took another deep breath. "I'm at the ranch. With Dad. And Kasey. And Beth."

When I was overseas I told myself this at the time at night when I tried to sleep. Im home. I'm at the ranch. With Dad and Kasey and Beth and Lee and Jamie. Expect now Lee is dead and Jamie's not around.

"I'm at the ranch. I'm home. With dad and Kasey and Beth." I closed my eyes and really made myself focused. "With Rip and Llyod and Jimmy and Walker and Clint and Colby and Ryan."

I opened my eyes. I was okay. So I took off again and trotted over the hill. I saw my dad sitting on a horse next to Kasey. I rode down to them. They stopped their conversation immediately.

"I thought I told you to take a break from wranglin'." Dad grumbled.

I sighed,"I ain't wranglin'. I'm here as a Dutton."

He nodded. "Good. Then there's something we need to talk about."

10

Dad didn't think the fires and alfalfa we're started by the Indians wanting to build the casino. It went against everything they believed it. Kasey suggested it was the people wanting to build the airport next to it.

We were all at home that night, eating dinner. As a family.

Gator made my favorite, country fried steak and mashed potatoes. He sat down the food.

I smiled up at him,"Have I told you how much I missed your cookin'?"

He sat down the collard greens and biscuits,"You haven't told me, but I assumed so because you're about to eat everything outta that kitchen."

Kasey chuckled,"I did the same thing when I came home."

"Is there beer in there?" I asked Gator.

"Yeah, I'll grab you one." He walked back.

"At the dinner table?" Dad looked pissed.

"What?" I asked as Gator sat down my beer,"Thanks, Gator."

He ruffled my hair,"Good to have you home, kid."

It started out as a quiet dinner but I couldn't stand the silence.

"Kasey thinks the airport people started the fires." I looked at Beth.

She stopped half bite.

"Mary." Dad gritted through his teeth.

My knife and fork clinked against my plate involuntarily. "For fucks sake, Dad, Beth needs to know too."

Beth nodded and finished chewing. "Yeah, as your lawyer and your daughter."

"Not at dinner." He shook his head.

I heard Kasey sigh.

"Well, what the hell are we suppose to talk about?" I laughed in a confused way.

"I say we talk about getting help at the bunkhouse. Rip needs few more wranglers. Especially after this mess. We've got thousands of acres of fence to put back up." Kasey butted in.

I looked at him and nodded. Thank you. I mouthed.

I grabbed my beer and took a long drink.

Dad grunted and stuffed potatoes in his mouth. Then he nodded. "I think you're right. And since Mary's done with being down there, he'll need the hel-"

I nearly choked on the liquid,"What?" I asked loudly.

Dad dropped his head,"We talked about this."

I sat my bottle down with a loud noise. "You said take a break, not quit-"

"Don't say quit like you worked there." He grumbled again and continued eating.

I looked at Kasey, terrified that my wrangling career was over. He looked up at our father who wasn't looking at any of us. Beth had a concerned look on her face, but was still lost because of the conversation that had ended abruptly about the airport people.

I stood up from my chair and grabbed my hat. "You said it yourself, Dad. I was in hell. And when I was there, all I thought about was wranglin' because that was my heaven. And you're taking it too." I nodded, pissed. Fuck finding peace with myself, this was cruel.

His silverware crashed onto the table. "Fine. Be a wrangler. But if you're gonna be one, be one. And we'll treat you like one. You know where the bunkhouse is." He nodded hatefully.

"Daddy-" Beth spoke up.

"No." He was breathing heavy, obviously pissed,"I made up my mind. She acts like a wrangler as it is. No manners. She cusses like one, chews and drinks and smokes like one, even at the goddamn dinner table. The military ruined her just like it did you." He cursed and stared straight at Kasey.

Kasey stood up abruptly. "That's enough-"

I put my hand on his arm. "It's okay." I whispered to him.

"Its gonna have to be okay. I want you out by dark. Kasey if you wanna argue, then go with her." My father stood up and stormed out.

I did the same and ran upstairs.

I grabbed my army duffle and started shoving my clothes and stuff into it. I grabbed M16 and my rifle and stuffed it in there. Then I put my pistol behind my back and tossed all my ammo in.

The door creaked open. It was Beth.

She sat on my bed and watched me pack.

"I finally got to wake up and see my little sister everyday." She grabbed my hand and squeezed it. I stopped pack and looked up at her. Her eyes were glossy,"But I knew it wouldn't last much longer. You always caused trouble and our father fucking hates trouble."

I giggled,"I'm sorry, Beth."

"Don't be sorry." She whispered then let go of my hand. "It was feeling too nice and normal around here. We need the change." She stood up and started to walk out. "By the way, the airport people would wanna burn everything that way the ranch showed a loss for this year." She whispered again.

I nodded, dropping the socks in my hand into the bag. "Okay. But why would they care if we had a big loss?"

She looked in the hallway then came back in,"If we show a loss, they can use it against us. Saying our land isn't making us money so we don't need the land. Just another reason for them to take it."

I nodded slowly.

"Come up here and see me when you can. I ain't going down to that damn bunkhouse just to see you. That place makes me want to cause trouble." She hung on the doorway.

I chuckled,"Yeah, well it always gets me in trouble."

"Goodnight." She winked then slipped out.

"I love you." I said out loud. It wasn't something my family ever really told each other. But we should start.

She looked back into my room. "I love you too, Mary." She gave a small, sweet smile and walked off.

11

I packed my bag over my shoulder and made my way to the bunkhouse. I could hear the music and hollering a ways away.

I pushed open the door and made my way in.

"Hey, it's cowboy!" Ryan teased.

They were all gather around the table, playing cards and drinking beer, their normal habitat.

I walked all the way in. They all saw my duffle. The laughing and talking stopped.

"Everything okay?" Jimmy asked quietly.

I walked over to an empty top bunk and threw my duffle on it. I took my hat off and put it on the rack. Then I opened the fridge and grabbed a beer. I pulled up a chair and sat down beside him.

My beer opened and foam oozed out,"You know, Jimmy," I took a long drink, everyone still silent,"I've never been better."

Everyone smiled and some chuckled. They started dealing out another game of poker and I joined in this time.

*****

Being the only girl in the bunkhouse was strange at first. But I realized soon it was just like the army but a little better. The beds were more comfortable and the company was consistent. Never dying or quitting. And these men didn't try to look at me when I changed or showered, even though I didn't mind if they did because I was so used to the army where all the men were as horned up as a dog in heat. I was the only girl those men saw other than towel heads with chlamydia.

The best part, was that my nightmares respected my space. I still had them and they were still terrible but I never woke up holding a gun to the door or screaming and yelling for back up. But I had other problems.

One night they all went out to the bar but I stayed back. I had a splitting headache. I laid down in bed and slept. Actually rested for once.

But I heard a door open and I felt someone grabbed my shoulder.

It was a quiet night. And hot. It was always hot. One of my private sat by the stone wall, keeping watch so Jake and I could rest. I stared at the white embassy building, with occasionally spots of black and brown were bombs were thrown at it. And soon I drifted off.

Then I heard shuffling. And talking. And I felt a bead of sweat rolled down the side of my face. Then yelling. Then I felt someone grabbed my shoulder. I jumped, afraid it was Jake, and something had happened. I was half right. Something had happened but it wasn't Jake grabbing me.

A man in black robes straddled my waist, waving a knife at me.

I grabbed my pistol down by my leg and pulled it up to his face.

Suddenly it wasn't his face. It was Jimmy. I think it's Jimmy.

"Whoa whoa whoa, hey!" I heard someone else yell.

Then more shuffling,"Don't try to take it from her, you'll make it worse." It was Lloyd. Maybe. It just sounded like him. Could've been anyone.

I stared at the person in front of me.

"Hey," the person looked calm,"Mary, it's Jimmy. It's me. And you're home." He spoke softly.

I blinked a couple times. Jimmy's face came into my vision. My finger fell off of the trigger.

"Good," He nodded when he saw it,"It's okay. It's me. It's okay." He stood off to the side and put his hand on top of the gun, slowly lowering it. I let him.

Then he grabbed it from me slowly and handed it to Lloyd who was behind him.

I huffed a short breath out. "I-Im so-" I stuttered and reached for him.

He leaned over and wrapped his arms around me like I wanted,"No, no, no it's okay. It was my fault. I knew better than to wake you like that."

I put my forehead to his chest.

He rubbed my back slowly until I calmed down. When I looked up everyone was doing their own thing. If they were phased by what happened, they weren't showing it for my sake.

I let go of Jimmy and sighed,"How was the bar?" I asked.

He chuckled,"I was waking you up to tell you that Colby got hit on by some crazy chick with pink hair."

*****

Maybe a month had gone by and I only spoke with my father a few times. And it was always about cattle or the ranch. Never anything personal.

Every day was hard and I liked it. It was mostly just fixing fence for a long time. But Rip was even harder on me. I'm assuming per my fathers request. But the hardest was not falling for him. He was tough on me and sometimes just harsh but I knew it was for my own good. I just couldn't get over how he worked. He looked so damn good working.

He was confident and tough. He knew what he was doing and did everything so well. I loved watching him work with the cattle no matter what it was. He loved those cows. But I also loved watching him get onto the other wranglers. I loved seeing him get pissed at them. He cuss them and it would make my heart skip beats. I sound crazy, but that's what everything was. Crazy.

Everyone was heading down to the rodeo one night. I showered with my good shampoo and curled my dark hair and put on a little make up. Then I picked out my best wrangler jeans. They had a small hole by one of the back pockets but I didn't mind. I ran the belt through the loops of my jeans and secured it with my 1st place healer roping buckle. I put on a burnt orange and turquoise pearl snap with a denim jacket over it. I slipped on my ostrich boots and put on my straw hat instead of my dirty tan one.

We all piled up in a few trucks then took off.

"Rip say he was coming later?" Lloyd asked from the back seat.

Ryan shrugged,"He said he would but you know how he is."

I mentally rolled my eyes. I was going to the rodeo to pick out a good cowboy for that night but of course Rip would come out tonight. The one night he actually goes out.

12

- -

The rodeo had the most energy I had seen at one in a long time. This was my first one since I came back home. And everybody wanted to say hi. Which I didn't mind. I had missed everyone. But everyone also wanted to buy me a beer. And I couldn't say no.

"Mary, how the hell are ya?" Wes, a boy I went to school with grabbed my shoulder when I was standing by one of the gates.

"Hey!" I turned around and gave him a quick hug, "I'm alright. You? Heard you got fucking married?" I elbowed him. Then looked around him. A tall man stood behind him, with a light brown short beard and a big cowboy hat. He was cute.

He chuckled, "Yeah, I can't believe it either." I was still looking around him, up the the stranger. "Alright then. Mary, this is Johnathon." He stepped out of the way.

Johnathon smiled at me and tipped his hat with his hand, "Howdy."

"Texas." I smiled softly.

"Pardon?" He leaned down a little to hear me over the roaring crowd.

"You're from Texas. Ain't nobody else do that hat tippin' thing." I gestured to the ten gallon on his head.

He chuckled,"Yeah, you're right."

We just stared at each other for a few seconds. A peaceful stare.

"Well, that was easier than I thought it was gonna be. I'll see ya around, Mare." Wes patted my back and walked off.

We both laughed awkwardly.

"You want a beer?" He asked.

Fuck. Not really. I've already half a fucking semi full.

But I smiled and nodded,"Yeah. I do." He bought me a beer and we stood behind the gates of the bronco riders, watching his younger brother.

"So, Johnathon, what do you do for fun? I'm assuming rodeo?" I teased. "Let me guess," I turned around and put my back to the cattle panel fence. I looked to my right and up to look him into the eyes,"Bull riding?"

He chuckled and took a long drink of the bottle beer, then he looked down, with taunting eyes,"No. Actually I think these things are a waste of time and money."

I nodded,"Well... you caught me off guard. That's a hell of an answer." I took a few slow blinks.

He smirked. "Just being honest. I don't have time for any way. And after working all the day, the last thing I wanna do is ride a fucking bull."

I chuckled,"I understand. What do you do for work?"

I took a drink out of my beer. I was expecting he would say construction or pipeline welding, maybe even lineman work.

"I break horses at a place called Four Sixes in Texas."

I choked on my beer.

"Are you okay?" Jonathon put his hand on my back.

"Fucking hell, man." I coughed. "You work at the Four Sixes?" I asked my eyes wide.

"Yeah, you heard of it?" He rubbed my back for a second then dropped his hand. I wish he wouldn't have stopped. It felt nice.

I laughed, "Wes didn't tell you my last name, did he?"

Johnathon looked confused, as he would be.

"My names Mary Dutton."

His eyes then went as wide as mine were. "Yellowstone, Dutton?" He asked. I nodded and laughed. "Damn, small world." He laughed too.

Then we were just staring at each other, smiling. The beer was making my head spin so I leaned back against the gate for support. He put his hand on the gate beside my head.

"You know, I should probably leave then." He said quietly.

I nodded, "Oh yeah?" I blinked slowly and looked into his brown eyes.

He pressed his lips between his teeth, nodding with me, "Without a doubt. Your daddy would have a hit out on me if he knew I was trying to get with his daughter."

"Lucky for you," I took a sip from my beer, "I don't give a shit what my father thinks."

He raised his eyebrows, "Really? That's the first I've heard from a Dutton." He lifted my hat up just a little, to look at me.

"Well," I put my hand on his chest and smooth out the wrinkle in his button down. The man wasn't wearing a vest or coat. Just the button down. I was in multiple layers and just barely warm enough. "We don't have nothing in common, I just happened to have the same name."

He leaned back and un buttoned the buttons by his wrist and started to roll up his sleeves. It revealed a tattoo on one side. A SEALS tattoo.

"You were a seal?" I asked.

"I was overseas with Kasey." He said quietly.

I nodded slowly and started to bring up my military career. But as soon as I did, he would know about the embassy takeover and it would just be awkward. We eventually went and sat down on the bleachers by the gates. So for the next couple of hours, we talked about anything but military, which only left cattle and horses. But there wasn't a quiet moment.

"Cowboy! We're heading back!" Ryan called over to me when the rodeo was almost over.

"Hang on!" I hollered back.

"Cowboy?" Johnathon chuckled and questioned.

"Long story." I smiled. "I guess I gotta go." I stood up.

He stood up too. "You sure? I don't mind to drive you home when we're done here." He grabbed my hand softly.

I looked down at it and smiled. Then I looked up at him and nodded. "I'd like that."

"You coming, cowboy?" Colby jogged over to me.

I stayed looking at Johnathon,"Y'all go on. I'll find a way back."

He looked at Johnathon then at me. "Alright, holler if you need anything." He patted my shoulder then headed towards the Yellowstone trucks.

Later when the rodeo was over, we were helping his brother finish loading everything.

"Alright, I'm taking off. Nice to meet you, Mary." His brother tipped his hat at me and walked off.

"He's friendly." I jumped up on Johnathons tailgate.

"Can be." He chuckled then walked up to me. He stood between my leg and leaned in.

Then around me to open his cooler and grab a couple beers.

"Want one?" He smirked.

I threw my head back laughing. He reached around and put his hand on my lower back, as if he was concerned I would fall backwards. "No, actually I don't!"

He took a long drink outta his beer then sat it on the bed rail. "Then what do you want," He took off my cowboy hat and sat it next to us,"Ms. Dutton?"

"Please Johnathon, call me Cowboy." I teased as he leaned into me.

He smiled against my lips as we tried to kiss but started laughing instead. Partially from the alcohol and partially from pure bliss. I felt happy.

"If I'm calling you cowboy then you better start calling me John. Because the only person that calls me Johnathon is my mother." He smiled and held my face with one hand. I stared into his green eyes.

"My mother died when I was younger." I spilled out.

His smile slowly faded into a caring, sweet frown,"I'm sorry to hear that." He brushed my hair over my shoulder. "It's hard to go on without a parent. I lost my dad last year."

I heard horses being loaded into trailers in the distance and men laughing. But here we are, being sad.

"Mary, I'm not gonna act like I haven't heard about you," He let out a sigh and dropped his hand from my lower back and sat it flat on the bed of the truck behind me, causing him to be closer. "I didn't know you were Mary Dutton when Wes introduced us but I've heard about you." He whispered.

I dropped my head,"About Afghanistan?" I asked.

"Yeah." He took both hands and comb my hair down then held my face. I sat there, expecting the sob story. The whole thank you for your service, you're so brave, you went through so much, I can't you are able to be standing here blah blah bullshit. But he caught me off guard. "You're a badass." He teased.

I laughed and shoved his hands away playfully. "I don't know. It didn't go as planned."

He grabbed my hand and rubbed the top of it with his thumb. "From everything I've heard, you did the best you could. None of that was your fault." He spoke softly.

I swallowed hard. "I lost too many men. And hundreds of innocent civilians."

He released a breath,"I walked a platoon into a mine field. And then we were attacked. We lost nine men." He had my full undivided attention. All I could do was stare and listen. "I blamed myself for years. But you can't live like that, Mary. It'll ruin your life. Trust me. I almost let it ruin mine." I didn't say anything. I didn't know what to say. "It almost seems impossible but you gotta separate your life over there from over here. That's not your job anymore. And that's exactly what it was. A job. You did your job." He brushed my hair out of my face again,"But they shouldn't have left y'all there by yourselves." He whispered.

I nodded and took in a shaky breath. "I, uh-" I cleared my throat, wondering if I should even go on talking,"I remember when we got the call that they were going to lift everyone out from the other stations in 36 hours. And that we would be the last ones for 12 hours. Fuck, we were only suppose to be alone for 12 hours." I lifted my hat off my head and rubbed my forehead then sat my hat back down,"But there was movement in the village 28 hours until the other platoons left. So my private and I went and camped." I sniffled, thinking of Jake. "He was new." I smiled and looked up at Johnathon who gave a smile, understanding smile back. "And hell, he was excited. Wanted to be a sniper so bad for his next tour." I swallowed hard again. "Anyway, we uh, we waited out. And-" I let out a shaky breath. "And it was 18 hours til the others would leave. We were about to leave and I saw movement." I blinked and briefly saw the child that I shot that night. "It was a kid." I nodded and looked at Johnathon. He was hanging onto every word. "Holding something... anyway I had to shoot him. And Jake was upset. As he should be, the kids are the hardest. But I was waiting for the retrieval and nothing happened. So we radioed out. And never heard from the land team. I thought maybe we were disconnected or they already left. But I found out when we came home that uh,"I nodded and looked up at him. He already knew.

"They were the team that was killed?" He asked. I nodded nervously still. The alcohol was helping me speak. I was never able to talk about these moments.

"Yeah, and I never put it together until recently that they happened killed Land team and then came up for Jake and me. And I still don't know why they just didn't take us all prisoners. Just Jake and me." I shook my head, still trying to wrap my head around it.

"They're fucking crazy out there." Johnathon mumbled.

I chuckled a little,"Tell me about it. They literally drug me and Jake to their station. Fuck, it wasn't a station. It was a goddamn hole in the side of a fucking mountain." He chuckled too. I paused. I was going to tell him what happened after that but I froze. "They're cruel people." I whispered. "Just cruel." My voice cracked. "And by then we were suppose to be heading home. And I wish,"I let out a short breath,"My platoon would've just left. They could've went home without us. And I wish they would have. Jake fucking died anyway and I was damn near close." I shook my head, talking to myself at this point, forgetting Johnathon was even around. "Instead they all fucking stayed and looked for us. By the time the fucking found us though, all platoons were gone and we had no one. So of course the fucking hadjis we're gonna take the embassy. There was no one to protect it. And we had to go fight for it back. But it was just us. I mean, what the hell could we do either the few people we had? And they wouldn't answer us. We made it inside the embassy at one point and called them one of the generals on a fucking dead guys cell phone to get help." I looked at Johnathon. He was nodding. Like he understood.

"I don't know why they were gonna leave y'all there anyway. It was bound to happen as soon as everyone else left." He huffed.

I nodded, "We should've all left at once, never been there to start with, or fucking stayed until all of the some bitches were dead." I finished the rant released a deep breath. I put my hand on his chest and tried once again to smooth out the wrinkles in his shirt.

"I know it doesn't mean anything from me, but when the news said that y'all took back the embassy and were holding it down. Just the few of you.

It made me proud to be a veteran." He wrapped his arms lightly around me. Just holding me softly. And I enjoyed it.

"I've never been able to talk about this all before." I whispered.

"Well, I like to think I'm a good listener." He teased.

I chuckled,"I doubt it. Doesn't seem like a trait most men have." I looked up at him longingly.

He chuckled and leaned in to try and kiss me again. I leaned back a little. He stopped.

"Is this okay?" He whispered. He held my face up one hand and grasped my lower thigh with his other.

I nodded,"Yeah... John." I smiled and our lips touched.

He lips were soft and warm. He tasted like beer and I loved it. My tongue slightly touched his and chills ran down my spine. I moaned into his mouth as he pulled me to the edge of the tailgate. I wrapped my arms around his neck and continued kissing.

"I would ask if you wanna come to my place but it's a bunk house full of guys." I said between kisses.

He chuckled,"My camper it is." He pulled me off the tailgate, still kissing. I wrapped my legs around his waist and he carried me to his passenger seat, never breaking the kiss.

The three minute drive to his camper was brutal. Soon we were stumbling up the metal stairs and into the extremely nice and huge four sixes camper.

Our clothing was disappearing piece by piece and by the time we made it to the bedroom, there was nothing to take off.

13

I t was 3am when I checked my phone and neither of us had slept. Not all from sex, mostly because we just kept talking. I rolled over back to Johnathon and rested my head on his chest.

"My brother and I gotta leave for Wyoming by 5." He kissed my forehead.

"It's a Sunday. I don't work Sundays." I stretched and snuggled down deeper into his and the blankets.

He rubbed my naked back,"Lazy bones." He chuckled. "I still gotta take you home."

"Yeah." I sighed. Not really wanting to leave my intended one night stand man.

"Or you could come to Wyoming." He said quietly.

I sat up and stared down at him,"What the fuck am I gonna do in Wyoming?"

He sat up too,"Break horses with me. You'll be good at it. Don't act like you don't wanna leave Yellowstone. You said it yourself, it's hell." He rubbed my shoulder.

I sighed and thought hard about it. "Maybe some day." I kissed his cheek.

"The offer will always be there, cowboy." He teased me.

We ended up falling asleep together and left way later then we intended. But we pulled up to the ranch around 6 and I gave Johnathon a last goodbye kiss and jumped out of the red Four Sixes truck. I opened the door to the bunk house and assume everyone would be up.

But no one was.

I grabbed a quick shower as quietly as possible the changed into fresh clothes. I normally didn't work Sundays but there were things I needed to get done. And I knew if I crawled into bed now I wouldn't be up until late this afternoon, wasting the day.

I heard someone stir and get up. It was Jimmy. He did work Sundays.

"Why are you up early?" He whispered, hoarsely.

"Couldn't sleep." I shrugged and slipped into my boots.

"You working today?" He asked and pulled a thermal shirt on.

I pulled a baseball cap on and my damp hair into a low bun. "Yeah, at least for this morning," I mumbled through the Bobby pin I held between my teeth. I pinned back some of the stray hairs. "We're getting new cuttin' horses next week and we need new corrals put up."

He buttoned up his shirt and put his carhart coat on. "Where we gettin' 'um from?"

I did the same with my jacket and we headed out the door as Walker and Lloyd were getting up.

"I don't know," It was a cold day and I regretted immediately washing my hair. I'll be sick with a head cold here soon. "Rip said Texas. Not sure where exactly."

Jimmy nodded and we got to work.

*****

It started raining around 4 so we quit early for the day. I took another shower and curled up in bed. When I was about to doze off over all the noise of the guys, I felt someone tap my shoulder.

"Let's go." It was Kayce.

I rolled over and stared at him. He looked nervous. "Go where? Kase, I'm tired. I didn't get home until late-"

"I'm serious, Mary." He mumbled under his breath then took off.

I rolled on my back and stared up at the ceiling, not wanting to get up. "Ugh." I sighed loudly and pulled myself up.

I jumped out of the bed and starting changing into real clothes.

"I think you gon have to start changing in the bathroom, girl. You gonna cause problems." I heard an unfamiliar voice speak.

Disgusted I turned around, with only jeans and a bra on,"Fucking pardon you?" I asked the ragged looking guy in the corner. He was maybe 30 and wore the same thing we all wore, jeans and a button down, dirty boots and a hat. He had a wad of chew in his mouth. He looked even worse than the last time I saw him.

"Names Keith." He spit the black liquid into an old Mountain Dew bottle. My stomach flipped. I knew exactly who he was.

"I know who you are perv," I pulled on a long sleeves and a hoodie, "Keep your dick in your pants this time or I'll rip it off like I promised." I stepped into my boots. By now, some of the guys over heard everything. Ryan was walking our way and so was Walker.

"As long as I get what I want first, I don't care how you play with it, baby." He smirked.

My blood boiled. I started to go after him but Ryan grabbed me by my waist.

"Hey, hey, hey not worth it!" He said while carrying me out the door.

"You fucking piece of shit! I swear to God I'll fucking kill you!" I was cussing the nasty man but I could still hear the jackass laughing.

Ryan sat me down outside. I was breathing hard and pacing. He was trying to calm me down. "He's an ass, I get it. But we need the help right now. And he's all Rip could find that knows what he's doing and won't rob us all-"

As soon as he said Rip I stopped. I opened my mouth then I saw Rip walking towards us from the barn.

I made a v line for him.

"Cowboy." Ryan said nervously. "Mary, don't!" He followed me quickly.

"What the hells going on-" Rip spat towards us.

He barely got it out before my fist connected with his jaw. "Fucking Keith?! I know we need the help but him?" I nearly screamed at Rip. I got ready to punch him again but Rip grabbed my arm. But not roughly.

"Hey, I know. I'm sorry." He whispered as blood ran out of his mouth. I wasn't expecting this.

I felt my whole body shaking. "You know what he did and who he is." I whispered back.

I heard Ryan walking away, back towards the bunkhouse.

Rip let go of my arm and wiped the blood from his mouth. "I know." He nodded. "I told him if he went anywhere near you he was dead. And I mean it." His eyes changed to dark colors.

I shivered, realizing I wasn't shaking from nerves, but from the cold. I only had my sweatshirt and long sleeves on. Not a coat or vest or anything. And the temperature was way lower than it was this morning. Rip must have noticed. He pulled off his coat quickly.

"I have to sleep next him." I said softly while slipping my arms into the coat.

"No you don't." He held up the jacket for me.

I crossed my arms once I was in it,"I can't go back to the house." I whispered.

"I know." He nodded. "You're gonna stay with me."

14

I stared at him. Relieved and pissed all at the same time. So many emotions were flying through all I could do was stare, straight faced at him.

He sighed. "I'll get some of your stuff later. We gotta go up to the cabin now. C'mon." He lightly put his hand on my back and gestured me forward.

I was shaky and nauseous from all the nerves. Then I panicked a little. I turned back and faced him, "I gotta find Kayce, he needed-"

He cut me off,"He's at the cabin."

I released a deep breath and nodded. Then continued walking. I looked up at him while we were walking. His mouth was still bleeding but he just stared straight ahead and ignored it.

"Sorry, boutcha lip." I spoke up.

A slow smile tugged on the corners of him mouth but quickly dropped. He stopped walking. I stopped too. "It's alright." Then he looked down at me,"But I don't like fighting." His voice was lowered and raspy. He had been smoking again but I didn't want to say anything, especially not now.

"You know what happens when someone gets in a fight around here. And I'll treat you the same damn way if this shit doesn't quit. I don't care how you did it in the fucking army." He started back up the hill towards the cabin and I quickly fell in behind him.

"You deserved it this time." I prayed he heard my teasing tone.

He chuckled. Thank god he chuckled. "You're right. I did."

I smiled and hugged myself tighter into his coat. It smelled like him. Just like his bed sheets and his t shirt. I was silently excited to be able to stay with while Keith was here. I would finally be able to sleep without nightmares and rest and feel safe again. Something I longed for since I stayed there that one night.

"Did you tell my dad about Keith?" I asked softly while we were walking.

"I did. He's okay with it."

My heart stung. My father knew who and what Keith was and was still okay with it. "Because I'm staying with you he's okay with it?" I asked in the same tone.

For the second time Rip stopped in his tracks. He shoved his hands in his pockets. "He doesn't know you're staying with me. I know he'll find out soon but I'll take the blame." He stroked his beard and looked around us. We were feet from his cabins front porch. "Because I can't let you stay in the bunkhouse with him."

My stomach had a tight feeling in it. I wanted to wrap my arms around his neck and buried my face in his chest. But I knew it wasn't a good idea.

Instead I smiled and put my hand on his chest. I patted him once or twice, "Thank you." Then I walked past him. I slid his coat off my back and sat it on the railing of his porch. Then I walked inside.

Kayce and Beth were sitting at the kitchen table, sipping whiskey.

"Where's Rip?" Kayce asked. I pointed to him as he walked in right behind me. "And Lloyd?"

I shrugged and opened my mouth to speak but "On his way." Came out of Rips mouth.

Good." Kayce nodded.

I leaned against the back of the couch,"Anyone wanna tell me what's going on?" I folded my arms. I was itching to smoke a cigarette as I watched Beth light one. I stared at it but realized Kayce was talking to me.

"-And they broke into the barn last night." I only caught the last part of the conversation.

"Wait, who did?" I asked.

Beth looked back at me,"Just some people. No reason to learn the names. They'll be dead soon." She took a sip of her whiskey. Lloyd walked in.

"The one's that wanna build the airport and casino?"

Kayce's eyes got wide and Rip looked quickly over to me. "Who fucking told you?" Rip spoke up.

I stared at him with hatred,"Word gets around-"

"That's enough." Lloyd interrupted our pissing match.

Kayce nodded,"She's known for a while."

I sighed and nodded,"Anyway, what did they want out of the barn?"Kayce, Rip, and Lloyd all stared at me like I was an idiot. "What?" I asked.

Rips face turned even more red and Lloyd looked at the ground.

"You weren't here last night, were you?" Kayce mumbled.

I swallowed hard. Fuck. I shook my head a little.

"Where the hell were you?" Lloyd spoke up for once.

"Nub uh." I cleared my throat,"What'd they take from the fucking barn?"

I felt Rip staring at me as I talked with Kayce about what all was taken. All medicines and vaccinations for the cattle. Beth explained why they wanted to take these. As we spoke I felt the heat of his eyes burning into me.

"Next time they're on our land, they're done." Kayce said quietly. "Enough is enough." He looked at me. "So make sure you're around if we need to shoot someone. Please." He shook his head and him and Beth walked out.

Lloyd and Rip were still staring at me.

I stared back. Not knowing if I should lie, leave, and just let them chew my ass out.

"I meet a guy at the rodeo and we got drunk. I got home this morning around 6." I shrugged as I walked to the fridge and grab a beer.

"Goddammit Mary, gimme one of those." Rip reached out to me. I handed him the one I opened for myself and grabbed a new one. He took a long drink and sat it on the counter with a loud clink. "You want to be a wrangler. You have to be here. It's your job."

My face turned red and I took a deep breath,"Then tell me what you tell the wranglers! Tell me about what goes on this ranch. One minute it's my ranch and I should act like it and the next I'm just a wrangler. Either fucking way, I should be told when there's people trying to steal our fucking land!"

Lloyd stood up from the kitchen table and stepped between us. He looked at Rip."She's not wrong-"

Rip shook his head and stormed out onto the porch before Lloyd even finished.

Pissed, I started to follow. Lloyd stopped me. "Let him go." He shook his head.

I looked around then took a few steps back.

"I don't even care about the fucking airport people anymore." I sat down at the table. "I don't know what the big deal is. The boys bring girls back to the bunkhouse all the time and he never says anything." I took a drink of the beer.

Lloyd sat down beside me. "Yeah, well they're not the little girl he use to take for rides on the four wheeler and help her shovel horse shit because she was too small to lift up the damn shovel and take care of her when she scrapes her knees after falling off the gate even though he told her she was gonna get hurt and show her what snakes are danger-" he went on and on.

I stood up abruptly,"I ain't that little girl anymore."

He stood up slowly. "Sit back down. I ain't done."

I swallowed hard, not knowing how to act. Lloyd hasn't spoke to me that way since I was a kid. I did as I was told.

He cleared his throat. "He wasn't much older than you but he knew a lot more. He had to grow up quick. And all he wanted to do was make sure nothing bad ever happened to you." He started to chuckle,"Like that time you and Lee and Kasey went fishing-"

"Oh lord." I started laughing too.

"You were gone for hours. And Rip was getting so nervous he couldn't stand it. He went out looking for y'all and he found ya alright." He was laughing now.

I smiled and shook my head,"Found me on a tree in the middle of the creek because I swam out to it and my dumbass couldn't get back."

Lloyd nodded,"I couldn't believe them boys left you there."

I chuckled,"They wanted to be home for supper in time."

"But Rip swam out there to ya and brought you back. Then beat the shit outta those boys." Lloyd finished the story. He looked at my beer and grabbed it. He took a drink from it. "My point is, Mary; He protected you for a long time. That was his job. Then you took off and he couldn't do it anymore." I nodded and stared at my hands, afraid to look over at him. "Then we heard on the news about the president pulling everyone out of Afghanistan. And we thought you were coming home." His voice cracked a little. I sniffled, remembering that I too thought I was going to come home. And how we had planned to be picked up the next morning. "And then we didn't hear from you. And no one could find you. And we thought we lost you for good."

I looked up at him. Tears whelmed in his eyes, causing my lip to quiver, fighting back tears.

"All I could think was; if we lose you, we'd lose Rip too. And he was different when you first left but man,"He shook his head,"When they told us you were stuck in that embassy building, he was a shell of a person. You didn't dare talk to him or ask a question or anything. We just let him be."

I glanced out the window. Rip was leaning on the railing of his porch, looking out towards the mountains and the ranch. Still looking like a mystery. The same mystery when I first came home.

Lloyd grabbed my hand that was on the table,"But you came home and he was back to normal. But he was mad that you left us all. He wouldn't admit it but he was. He was mad we almost lost you and he couldn't do anything to help protect you. That's why he's so hard on you. Because he's mad at himself. And now, all he wants to do is make sure you stay safe." He squeezed my hand then stood up.

He walked towards the door,"So for fucks sake, don't go around sleeping with people."

I let out a small laugh and brushed my tears away. "I'm sorry. It won't happen again."

He gave a small smile,"Well..." he grabbed the door handle.

"Thank you, Lloyd. For everything." I softly said.

He nodded then walked out. I watched him pat Rip on the back then walk off.

But Rip didn't come inside. Not for a long time. So I sat on the couch, curled up in a blanket, drink a glass of whiskey, and waited up for him. I didn't care that I had to work tomorrow morning and I hadn't slept in 36 some odd hours. I was use to the no sleep.

Later on the door creaked opened. Rip walked in slowly.

"Why are you still awake?" He grumbled.

"Waitin' on you." I sang.

He huffed,"Might be a while." He walked through and grabbed his truck keys.

"Why? Where are you going, Rip?" I asked hesitantly, afraid of his answer.

"To go find your lover boy." He mumbled and headed for the door.

I stood up quickly,"What?! No! Why?" I ran out the door after him. The cold air nipped me in the face.

"To kill him." He had made his way to the truck and opened the door roughly.

I grabbed the door before he could close it. "You don't even know who he is!"

He started the truck and it roared to life. "Its the 6666's guy. Now let go of the damn door." He was breathing heavy.

My jaw dropped,"How did you know?" I was a deer in headlights and almost as dead as one.

He sighed loudly and shut the truck back off,"Do I look like a dumbass?"

"You want the real answer?" It slipped out of my mouth before I could stop it.

He clenched his mouth shut. "I saw you and him together last night. I saw you all over him and I saw how he looked at you. He didn't just wanna fuck, he looked like- like he thought more of you." I didn't realize Rip ever showed up last night.

I swallowed hard and thought about what I was about to say,"Isn't that the kind of guy you would want for me to be with?"

His face softened. He stepped out of the truck and closed the door behind him. "He's from Texas."

"And?" I asked.

"I can't protect you if you're in Texas." He spoke up.

I lost it. Forgetting everything Lloyd just told me. "Then stop trying to protect me! I'm not a little girl anymore, Rip!" My voice cracked and I ignored nearly all advice Lloyd and I had just talked about.

He looked devastated. Like what I told him was new news that he had never heard of.

"Then why do you look to me every time you need help?" He stepped closer to me. "When I told you their were gonna be helicopters, you came straight up to me with this look in your eyes. Like you needed me." He reached up and put his hand on the side of my face. I clenched my jaw and wanted to shove his hand away and tell him not to touch me. But I didn't. "It's the same look you gave me that night I came over because of your nightmares. And the look you gave me earlier when I told you that you could stay with me." He rubbed his my cheek with his thumb and I was happy I didn't shove him away. It made me feel loved, something I didn't have a lot of recently. "I can't stop protecting you. I want to keep you safe. It's the one thing I'm good at. Don't take that from me."

I looked deep into his eyes. And prayed hard that he would leaned down and kiss me. But I thought about my father. And how he said I needed to get it through my head that Rip was just here to protect us all. It was his job. And I'm romanticizing it. I need to let it go.

15

Every day was busy between putting up corrals and running new fence. It felt like we would be putting up and fixing fence for years. I didn't mind the work but I also rather be with the cattle.

Colby, Ryan, and I were fixing the fence down in pasture 4 when Rip came riding up to us. I stopped what I was doing and looked out at him riding across the pasture.

"What's wrong?" Colby stood up and looked in the direction I did.

I shook my head,"I don't know. But something is." I started walking out into the pasture towards him.

"He's in a hurry." Ryan coughed and cleared the dust from his throat.

I stepped through the taller grass and walked a little faster. His horse clumped and clumped as it's hooves hit the ground.

"What's going on?" I asked as soon as I was close enough for him to hear me.

He didn't have his coat on, only his button down. And I was surprised because it was cold.

"I can't get a fucking horse out of a trailer." He cussed.

I released a deep breath. "Thank god."

"What the hell'd you'd just say?" He took the toothpick out from between his teeth.

"Nothing, just thought something was wrong." I chuckled and started to walk back towards the boys.

"I gotta get this horse out. We're paying those guys by the hour to bring them here." He dismounted his horse and followed close behind me.

"So? Get the horse outta the trailer?" I grabbed my wire cutters out of my pocket and went back to the fence.

Colby pulled the wire tight for me so I could twist it back together. "What's going on?" He grunted and asked at the same time, using his strength to twist the wire.

"Can't get a horse outta a trailer." I mumbled.

"Go ahead, cowboy. We're almost done here anyway." Ryan walked up to take my place. I stood up straight again and stared at the three of them.

"You want me to get him out?" I ruffled my eyebrows. "I ain't done that shit in years. Like almost 10 years." They all still stared at me. "I was a kid, guys. I don't know what I'm doing now." I shook my head.

"They said you were always great at-" Colby started.

Rip butted in, "I ain't got time to argue with you. Get your ass to the barn." He stomped away to his horse and jumped on. He stared at me for a second then rode off.

I sighed loudly.

"He's an ass to you." Ryan scoffed.

"Don't start. He's just kinda hard on me. I think it's per my fathers request." I chuckled and untied my horse from the fence post. Then I rode off to the barn as I was told.

From half a mile away my heart fell through my chest and down into my stomach. It started pounding and I felt like I couldn't catch my breath. But I smiled.

There was a red truck and a red trailer. And a tall, tan Texan standing outside of it.

I rode up quick and smiled wide as I saw John. I dismounted my horse and started walking his way.

"Cowboy!" He laughed and nodded at me.

"You missed me already?" I teased. "I heard you got a problem." I rested my hands on my hips. I saw Rip come out from the barn. My smile dropped. "If you wanna live, act like you don't know me." I said quickly and quietly.

"What?" He choked on his words.

Rip handed me a halter,"Mary, this is John. John, Mary."

I nodded at John and stuck my hand out,"Nice to meet ya."

He shook my hand back and nodded. He was confused but played along.

Rip walked towards the trailer and I heard the horse start to stir. Whimpering almost.

I followed close behind and looked into the trailer. "She's hurt." I mumbled.

"Speak up, girl." Rip bitched at me.

I faced him sharply,"She's fucking hurt."

He took the toothpick from between his teeth,"And? Get her out and we'll take care of her. We ain't got time for this."

"I don't mind to help her but You want us to keep an injured horse?" I spoke softly to Rip, hoping John wouldn't hear.

But he did. "She was fine when I left this morning. She ain't hurt." He glanced in the trailer.

I scoffed and looked up at him,"Bullshit. Listen to her." John ruffled his eyebrows at me. Then he just stared at me and listened. She whined and brayed softly. John shrugged and shook his head, not knowing what to think of the horse stuck in the trailer.

Rip shook his head,"I don't have fucking time for this. Get her out of there whether she's hurt or not." He turned to John. "You better not have brought me a fucked up horse."

John straight his shoulder and started to puff his chest. "I take care of these horses-" he took a step to Rip.

I put myself between them quickly and faced John. "Im not saying you don't. She could've easily turned an ankle in the trailer. Just help me get her out." He looked down at me. Breathing heavy. I looked up into his eyes and blinked slowly.

He was even more attractive than I last remembered. I wanted to push my lips onto his and throw myself onto him. But now wasn't the time. Especially with Rip standing behind me.

He unclenched his jaw and swallowed hard. Then nodded. "Yeah."

I heard Rip shuffled behind me. He knew something was going on.

I hurried over to the trailer and slowly opened the door back up.

"Hey, girly." I spoke to the beautiful cutting horse. She was lean but muscular. Her hair was shiny, showing she was well fed with good nutrients.

She scuffled a little but wasn't scared of me. I stepped into the trailer. She was favoring her front left hoof. Looked like part of it had been caught on something.

"Mary, get your ass out of there. She's been jumping around." Rip mumbled quietly.

"She's not gonna hurt me." I whispered softly. "Are ya? You just don't feel good." I said with sympathy. "What's her name?" I asked John.

"Trigger."

I stopped and turned to him. "It's a girl."

He smiled,"The old man that trained her said she's as stubborn as a trigger finger. Kinda stuck."

I smiled. "Trigger? No wonder you're pissed." I teased the horse. She stopped moving and looked right at me. She knew her name.

I took a couple steps forward.

"Mary, you're gonna get pinned." Rip spoke up a little.

"Only if you scare her." I whispered and took another step. "You still train them by bridles?" I asked John another question.

He stuttered,"Uh, yeah. We do. How'd you-"

"Don't ask." Rip huffed. He saved me from the long conversation I was not ready to talk about with John.

I was within feet of her bridle. If I could grab it, she would know I was in control and she would feel safe. And she'll walk right out of here.

I took another stepped. She picked her feet up and stammered quickly but in one spot. I froze and waited.

"This is enough. Get the fuck out of there." Rip gritted through his teeth.

"'Cowboy, he's right. She's gonna buck. She's done it before." John took Rip's side.

"I'm fine-"

"How the fuck do you know they call her cowboy?" I heard Rip speak up.

"I've heard plenty of stories." John chuckled, trying to lighten the mood. But it different work. Rip took it the wrong way. I heard shuffling.

"Is this the guy?" Rip hollered towards me.

"Rip-" I turned to look at him but he grabbed John by the collar, who was holding the trailer door. The door slammed shut and Trigger decided that was enough.

I heard her bray as I turned, wide eyed. She tried to stammer and buck but had no room. She jumped and shook the trailer. I stumbled to keep my balance and I heard someone yell my name. It was Kayce.

Then I watched Trigger try to turn herself around but became agitated when she didn't have much room. She pushed her body against the side of the trailer. It moved the entire trailer and I assumed the truck but I couldn't see it. It took me to my knees and I hit the ground. All I could do was cover my head and pray.

I heard the boys yelling about the door being stuck and Kayce yelling for me. Suddenly she stopped jumping. Then I felt a big, wet nose nudge my arm. I slowly looked up. She was concerned about me. She pushed her big head against my shoulder. I smiled and rubbed her nose and forehead. I stood up slowly.

The trailer door flung open.

"Mary." Kayce released a deep breath and reached out for me to come to him. I looked at him then at Trigger. I grabbed her bridle and walked her out slowly. She complied and stepped out of the trailer with me.

I felt everyone's eyes on me but I was just focused on the giant creature that was worried about me. I scratched her jaws then led her into a pin.

And she trotted around like she was happy, but still favoring the hoof. We'll wrapped it up later. I released a deep breath.

"Are you okay?" Kayce put a hand on my shoulder. I turned to him and nodded.

"Just a little shook up." I buried my face into his chest and wrapped his arms around me and squeezed.

"Scared the hell out of me." He let go of me.

"Me too. I'm so sorry about her. I thought we broke her of that a long time ago. I'll bring y'all another horse. Won't even charge to take this one back and bring another." John put a hand on my shoulder.

I shook my head,"No. We'll keep her. She's smart."

"Are you sure? I don't mind-" Johns eyes were full of worry.

I smiled a small smile. "Really, John. It's okay."

Kayce looked at me then back to John. Then back to me. Then he smiled. "I'll let you two catch up." I blushed. He stuck his hand out and shook Johns hand,"Good to see you again, brother."

"You too, man." John nodded and chuckled. I smiled until I saw Rip stomp away. My smiled dropped. I released a deep breath. "You ain't got a boyfriend, right?" John teased.

I chuckled and shoved my hands in my pockets. Then I looked out into the setting sun. "Not yet." I winked.

I walked him around the ranch even though he had been here before, just not when I was here. The sky was an orange red color. A sunset you don't normally see in Montana. But it was familiar. One I had seen millions of times. I stared out at it.

"Looks like a desert sunset." John shoved his hands in his pockets.

I sighed,"I was just thinking that." I looked around then just sat down in the prairie grass where we were standing. He sat next to me. Close.

"It's a hell of a lot prettier when you're standing in US soil." He nudged me.

I chuckled. "It definitely is. Nice to just enjoy it and not be shot at."

He matched my laugh but it faded. "I feel like I ain't seen ya in years." His Texas accent rang through my ears and made me melt a little.

"It's only been a few weeks." I teased.

He nodded,"I know. But I think about you everyday." He whispered and out of the corner of my eye I saw him turn his head and big hat to me.

I looked at him. I could've said something sweet like I thought about him too. Hell, I should think about him. He's one of the most attractive men I've ever seen and we have so much in common. And sometimes I did think about him but not everyday. I was too busy to. I should've told him I would go with him to Texas this time. But I couldn't think of anything good to say.

"Good." I winked and smiled.

He shook his head and squinted his big eyes. "I'm being serious. It gets me in trouble."

I took my ball cap off and tossed it in the grass. I ran a hand through my dirty black hair. "Mmm I like trouble." I teased him again and again.

"I tried hooking up with a girl last week." He said bluntly.

I bit my tongue between my teeth.

What the fuck.

I scoffed, "Alright, you got me. Not that kinda trouble."

He chuckled and put his hand on my leg and squeezed my thigh, "I couldn't though. Just kept thinking about you."

It was a weird thing to hear and an even weirder thing for him to admit. But it made me feel good. I smiled a small smile. Happy with how he made me feel comfortable and relaxed. "You're crazier than hell." I shook my head.

He looked out at the dark, snow covered mountains and the now darkening sky. "Sweetheart, you got in a trailer with a pissed off horse today."

I leaned my head on his shoulder, "If you think that's crazy, you ain't seen nothing yet."

He let out a little huff, "Oh what have I done." He rested his head on top of mine.

We stayed out in the pasture for long than planned. But I couldn't bring myself to leave him. We stood at his truck and trailer, making out for over thirty minutes.

He pulled away from my kiss, even though he had me pin to the truck driver side door. "I gotta go." He whispered.

"Why?" I pushed my lips back to his. He kissed me once and broke away again.

"Babydoll, I gotta be in Colorado by tomorrow morning and I'm already gonna be late." He rubbed my cheek with his thumb. I sighed leaned back against the truck. I smoothed his shirt down and then patted his chest.

I looked up at him. "I don't think you should go."

"I think you should come with me." He said immediately. He smirked because he knew I was thinking about it.

I shook my head,"John we've talked about this." I sighed.

He kissed my forehead softly. "I hope they all don't treat you how he did today. It's gotta be miserable."

I leaned back and looked up at him. "Who Rip?" He nodded. It kind of pissed me off. He doesn't know Rip enough to say that. And I almost told him that. But instead I just sighed and rolled my eyes,"He's just tough on me because my dad told him to be. He treats me like he treats everyone else."

John again nodded slowly, noticing my hostility,"I still don't like it. I wouldn't ever talk to you like he did."

I shrugged. "I grew up with all that. From my brothers, dad, other wranglers. Just how we talk here, I guess."

I heard a coyote howl miles away. But closer than normal. I listened closely. Just the one right now.

John was listening too. "You're gonna be up all night now, huh?" He teased and squeezed my arm.

I chuckled and wrapped my arms around his neck, deciding to forget about everything he said. "If you stay, I'll keep you up all night too." I planted a kiss of his lips.

"Hmmmm, that sounds nice." He wrapped his arms around me and dropped his hand down to my ass and squeezed. I smiled into him and he did the same. "Im leaving." He smack my ass quickly then let me go.

I smiled and folded my arms, watching him get in the truck. "Be careful." The words rolled off my tongue. Something a girlfriend would say to her boyfriend or a wife to a husband.

He smiled. "Just for you." Then he winked and started the truck. It roared to life and I watched as he pulled away slowly.

I immediately felt lonely. I sighed and started walking to the bunkhouse just to realize I wasn't staying at the bunk house and walked the long walk to Rips cabin.

I heard more and more coyotes, closer and closer. Too close. I walked up onto the steps of the cabin then opened the door. Rip wasn't on the couch and I didn't hear the shower. I grabbed my rifle by the door then stepped back onto the porch and down the hill. I opened the door into the bunkhouse, everyone was quiet and calm for once.

"I'm gonna check on some coyotes." I stuck my head in and told them.

Jimmy looked up from his beer and grabbed his hat from the table,"I'll go with ya."

I nodded. Then shivered. Keith stepped out of the bathroom with just a towel around his waist and walked over to his bunk. He pulled something out of his bag and dangled it.

A pair of red women's panties. My panties. That were in Rips house.

I swallowed started and tried to step through the door.

Suddenly Jimmy walked quickly towards me,Let's go." Jimmy grabbed my shoulders and stopped me. I tried to brush him off but he was stouter than he looked. I jerked my head up to him,"He's not worth it. C'mon, go." He pushed me back a step or two. I stopped resisting him but just stared.

I clenched my jaw. Keith dropped them back in his bag and chuckled. "I'm gonna kill him." I whispered.

"I know, cowboy. Come on." He rubbed my arm and started to turn me around.

I became nauseated and started sweating. The kind of nerves that cause your face to get hot and make your head dizzy flooded my whole body.

I let myself listen to Jimmy. I nodded and walked back through the threshold. I started towards the barn but stopped halfway. My mouth got watery. I tried to ignore it. But I couldn't. I felt vomit rising up in my throat. I leaned over and starting throwing up. I rested my hands on my knees and prayed I didn't get anything in my hair that was flying around due to the wind.

Soon I felt Jimmy's hand on my back. "I'm sorry." He whispered. But I could barely hear him. I just kept getting sick.

If only John were here now.

"I don't know why he's still here." I quickly said and gasped for a breath between dry heaving. Jimmy didn't say anything. Just kept rubbing my back. I spit the left over saliva out onto the ground. It hit the dirt with a plop sound. "How did he even get those out of Rips cabin?" I sniffled and blinked the watery tears out of my ears. I was only crying for the fact that I threw up all of my insides and my eyes watered bad when I did so. He still didn't say anything. And I guess I wasn't really looking for an answer, just needed to get it off my chest.

*****

"You find any coyotes or wolves?"

There was a knock at the door then I heard Rips voice. I groaned and then yawned. "No. Why the fuck are you asking now?" I rolled over in the bed and pulled the blankets up under my chin.

"I keep hearing 'em." He was quiet for a few seconds. "I'm gonna go check again." I heard him walk towards the dresser to grab jeans.

"Rip, it's fine. They're not anymore close. Just get some rest, you need it." I spoke softly and sleepily. I was basically drunk at this long due to the drowsiness.

I heard shuffling. And the draw opening and then closing. And the sound of him putting his belt on. Then he was out of the room.

I sighed and rolled over, falling back asleep quickly.

This went on every night for maybe a week. Wolves were close but never too close. It really wasn't anything unusual. But Rip was on edge about something with the cattle. He also never spoke unless it was about the cattle. We had our knock out drag down about John and how I lied and acted like I didn't know him. We fought about it but never really resolved anything. It was a sensitive subject and we just chose not to speak of it.

Once again, I was curled up asleep in bed when I heard heavy foot steps. I sat up quickly and reached for my gun on the nightstand. I had it drawn to the door when someone walked in through the threshold.

He glanced at me and opened his arms. "Mary." He said softly.

I stared. I know him. I think. Try and think. I kept staring.

"Mary, come on, girl. Put it down." He had an accent that rang through my ears. It was comforting. And sounded like home. "It's Rip, darling. You know who I am. I'm not trying to hurt you."

I released half of a deep breath. "Rip?" I whispered and blinked hard. It was him. I just hadn't recognized him. I slowly lowered my pistol.

"It's me. Put it down, babe." He whispered. I nodded and dropped the gun onto the bed. He quickly walked over and grabbed it, then tossed it on the nightstand with a clanging noise. "You okay?" He asked.

"I think so." I mumbled. "I'm sorry." I rubbed my eyes with the heels of my hands.

I felt his eyes on me. "Are you sure?" I nodded. He put his hand on my back. For the first time since our blowup about John, he didn't look pissed at me. "I'm gonna go check a pastures." He rubbed my back then turned to the dresser and grabbed a long sleeved shirt. It was getting extremely cold outside these past few days and had no plans of warming up.

Here we go again with the fucking wolves.

"What for?" I asked, expecting a smart ass answer.

"I don't know." He sighed, "Just got a bad feeling."

I was taken aback by his answer. It worried me a little.

I nodded. "Be careful." I closed my mouth as soon as I said it.

He looked back at me, confused. Almost as confused as I was. "Uh, yeah. I will be. Get some sleep." And he was out the door.

After this episode I couldn't sleep but a couple hours a night. Especially with Rip up and down all night every night. I was going on three solid nights with no sleep. Almost 78 hours at this point. It was something I did in the army quite a bit, but I was out of shape. My body hadn't been sleep deprived in months.

So after work I took a long shower. I didn't even go to dads to eat like I said I would. I just laid down in bed by 8:30. It was at least an hour before I doze off. But only for a few minutes. Because soon the front door slammed shut. And Rip came walking into the bedroom.

"Have you checked pasture 12 tonight?"

I didn't even move. I couldn't. I was so exhausted. Just mumbled,"Yeah."

And he walked back out. I dozed off again maybe an hour later.

But soon someone came stomping in,"Looks like bear tracks in the woods here by the bunkhouse. Make sure you keep an eye out for 'em."

"Alright." I mumbled again and yawned.

I thought maybe he was done of the night. That there was no way he would say anything else.

But boy was I wrong. He came in one last time.

"Did any of the pastures have tracks-"

All I wanted to do was sleep. I was so tired. I felt my face turning red and my heart thumping. I sat straight up. "For fucks sake, Rip! Would you just leave it alone?! I checked. It's fine out there!" I nearly cried out to him. He furrowed his eyebrows and opened his mouth to speak. "No! I checked every fucking pasture! They're fine! Now let me fucking sleep!" I ranted. He opened his mouth again. "I spent eight years without sleep. And I come home and all I want is a decent nights rest. I'm just now handling the nightmares but I can't get a damn minute of sleep in without you being worried about something. So stop! Goddammit, just let me sleep!" I released a deep breath I didn't now I was holding.

I was starting to wake up finally and realize I just completely flipped out on him. Maybe it was actually from lack of sleep, or exhaustion, or stress about Keith but probably about John leaving, I couldn't keep it in anymore. I finally lost it.

He stared at me. I thought he was gonna be mad but he looked concerned. And almost upset. He walked out of the bedroom.

"Rip, wait! I didn't mean-" I stopped when I heard the front door shut. I sighed and dropped my head. "Fuck." I mumbled. Ive done it. Ive pissed him off again.

*****

Later on the week and into the weekend, a bunch of us decided to go to the bars in town. Kasey even went with us and was the one to drop me off later than night. Or that next morning around 3am. I opened the door to the cabin and it creaked.

Fuck. I whispered in my head.

I watched Rip stir on the couch but fall back asleep and snore. I smiled at his snore and quietly walked through the house. I was more drunk than I realized when I stumbled and grabbed a kitchen chair for support but the chair tipped over onto the floor along with me.

Rip sat up from the couch and looked over at me on the ground. "What the fuck are you doing?" He asked loudly.

I giggled which turned into a laugh. "I fell." But I just sat there. The thought of getting up was hard enough, but trying to was going to be a whole new story. I watched Rip get up from the couch and walk my way.

He reached down and picked me up like an adult would a toddler and he sat me on my feet. I was unsteady and leaned away and then back to him. I rest my hands on my chest and he smiled.

"What did you drink?" He chuckled and tried to walk me to the bedroom, which seemed forever again.

"Uhhh," I took a couple steps but leaned into him more,"Beer. A lot of it." I giggled and kept trying to walk. I kept missing my step even with focusing on my feet super hard. I tripped a lot this time and started to fall dead weight. Rip caught me but we ended up against the hallway wall. He was close to my face. I stared into his eyes. He was looking back into me.

I glanced at his lips and wondered if I could kiss him. I know I'd like it and he would too.

But he interrupted,"Come on, girl. Let's get you to bed." He ignored everything that just happened.

*****

It was inevitable that things would escalate. Maybe we were both lonely or maybe it was because we spent so much time together. Spending all day working and then going home together. I was always back to the cabin before him so I would strip down on the porch to keep from getting the floors and everything else dirty. Then I would take a shower and start on fixing dinner. It was hard to adjust to just cook for us because I was so use to feeding the bunkhouse full of hungry, usually drunk men. By then Rip would be back. He always sat on the porch for a while. Always in silence, always drinking beer.

I became more comfortable around him again, like when we were kids and he would watch over me. I could lean on him again. This didn't change how things were while working though. He was still an ass most of the time but once again, my smart mouth didn't help any either.

"We gotta move these cows through that tree line." Rip hollered to us as we were getting our horses ready for the long, dusty ride. It hadn't rained or snowed in almost a week. It was going to be a fucking mess.

"Why don't we push "em over the mountain?" I asked as I saddled my horse. I was the last one to do so, I had been running late this morning because Rip didn't start the drier last night and I had no clean jeans.

He walked his horse up to me. "Is it gonna be like this all day?" He took the tooth pick from his between his teeth.

"Like what?" I tightened my straps then pushed the hair out of my face.

"You being a pain in the ass because I didn't start the dryer." He said quietly.

I mounted my horse and sighed. "It's not about that. I don't even care that I'm wearing jeans too tight that every time I get up on this gal, my ass has the opportunity to fall out-"

He opened his mouth to speak.

"Nah. Hang on. It's about the fact that I don't wanna get hit in the face with a thousand fucking tree limbs." I rolled my eyes and nudged my horse with my heels. I lifted my gator up over my face to help with the dust.

"Toughen up then. We're not going over that fucking mountain." He rode up next to me.

I pulled on the reins and stopped. I bit my tongue hard.

By now, Jimmy had slowed down from everyone else and was watching.

"Toughen up?" My voice shook.

"You're a fucking wrangler-"

"I was a fucking soldier." I raised my voice. I couldn't see his eyes through his sunglasses so I didn't know his emotions but I assumed they changed quick. "Don't tell me to toughen up." I scoffed. "You've said a lot of stupid shit,"I gritted my teeth together,"But this-" I shook my head and looked around. "That's bad, Rip. Even for you." I turned my horse around and trotted back to the barn.

"Where the fuck are you going?" Rip hollered after me.

"I'm taking a personal day!" I yelled back. I jumped down off my horse once I was out of view. I was breathing hard, pissed. I balled my fists.

Toughen up. You've got to be fucking kidding me.

I put my hands down onto a bale of straw in the barn. I leaned on it and rocked back and forth, trying to calm down and not let myself slip away. I felt it coming on.

I squeezed the straw hard, it hurt my hands a little but it felt good to feel something.

"Mary..." I heard Jimmy walk into the barn.

I looked up,"Hey. Sorry, you heard that." I wiped my face off, trying to catch a grip on myself.

He shook his head,"You're right. Those limbs are gonna tear the hell out of those cattle."

I looked at him. "You're not as stupid as you look." I chuckled.

He smiled,"Depends on the day."

I smiled back. "You wanna run some cows over a mountain?"

His eyes got wide,"The two of us?" I nodded. He shook his head and started to stuttered,"I really don't think, that's a... a good idea. You know, Rip would be pissed-"

I remounted my horse again,"That's the point Jimmy."

The herd was split into two. Although Rip was right and going through the tree lines would be easier since we were down people, but it could cause us to lose a cow or two. Going over to the mountain wasn't an easy ride, and if you didn't know how to control your horse, could end up in some serious injuries.

So when they took with their half, Jimmy and I were suppose to watch the other while we wait for them to come back.

Suppose to.

It wasn't pretty, and it wasn't a good idea, but we ran every cow over the mountain. The ride was rough and beat the hell out of the both of us. I was nervous about Jimmy, but he did great. As if he had been riding a horse since he was youngun.

We were running our cattle into the new pasture when I realized the other cattle weren't there yet. I chuckled to my self and shook my head. Rips gonna be really pissed.

All cattle ran right into the pasture full of clover for them, they hadn't been here since winter of last year, so it was new to them. One stray cow ran off so I followed her, roped her and brought her back.

Maybe thirty minutes later, the other cattle came through the tree line.

Jimmy and I helped.

Rip didn't say a word.

Until later that night.

We were all hanging out in the bunkhouse when Rip barged in. I already knew what he was there for.

"You want a beer?" I asked. He shook his head. I sighed and stood up. "I think I'm gonna need one." I opened the fridge and grabbed a Coors. Then I started to follow Rip out the door. I turned to the guys and folded my hands in prayer and jokingly pleaded to them to save me silently. Most chuckled but continued playing cards.

I cracked open my beer and foamed slowly rushing through the hole as we walked through the door way.

I closed the door shut with my boot. Rip knocked the beer out of my hand and gave me a shove against the door quickly. "Dude!" I shoved him back.

"Listen to me." He pointed to my chest and lowered his voice. "You pull the shit you pulled today again..." He shook his head.

"Then what?" I stuffed my hands in my pockets and leaned against the door.

"And you're done. I'm not putting up with this, Mary." His voice softened. And he sighed. "I want to work with you. I want you to be here to work cattle every day. Because goddammit, you're good at it." He let out a breath and turned to look out towards the mountains. "But we can't keep doing this. You're gonna have to decide if you're the owner, or the wrangler. Because doing both, ain't working out." He said with a breathy, exhausted voice.

I stared at him. He was right. I hated the sound of that. But he was.

"I don't mind being a wrangler. I don't mind you treating me as a wrangler. But when we go home at night, would you just listen to what I have to say. About the cattle. You know the mountain was. A better plan. You lost a cow today. And I didn't-"

"This is what I'm talking about." He started to raise his voice again. "We do things my way," He cleared his throat,"Or you do it your dads way."

My mouth hung open. "Rip..."

He shook his head and started to walk away.

"Wait-" I grabbed his arm. And I just held it. I liked how his arm felt. Lord, I sound crazy. I liked the warmth of him and the strong, safe feeling. It made me feel small. In a wonderful way. "You called me weak." I whispered.

He nodded,"I shouldn't of said it like that. And I'm sorry." He pulled his arm away and reached out to rub my shoulder like he did occasionally.

But I couldn't help it. I felt into him and wrapped my arms around his sides and squeezed. He draped his arms across my shoulders. He huffed a little, maybe even a small laugh. "Come on, now. Let's go home." He rubbed my back then let go.

It always stopped at a hug. Never anything more. Everytime we were any kind of intimate, it was only a soft touching of each other's arm or hand or face. And sometimes hugs. But never anything more. Kinda.

I got back to the cabin one day and stripped down. Then I walked in and tossed steaks into the sink to thaw. Then I slipped into the shower. When I finished, I reached out for a towel. But there wasn't one.

"Dammit, Rip." I mumbled. I opened the bathroom door, dripping water and naked as a jay bird, then looked out into the bedroom. No towel there.

I sighed then shivered from the cold air. I walked quickly into the laundry room and opened the dryer. Towels. Wet towels.

I cussed Rip again and slammed the door shut then started the dryer. I walked back towards the bedroom. By now, I was half way dry, at least my body, definitely not hair. I opened the chest of drawers and dug for a tshirt and shorts. Then my life flashed before my eyes.

Rip stepped into the bedroom. He was on the phone with what I was assuming the vet.

"I need you here, yesterday. It's a deep wound-" he looked over at me and his eyes widened. "Call you back." He hung up the phone. "Fuck, Mary- I'm sorry. I didn't realize-" he was torn between looking at me and looking away.

"Maybe, if you would start the fucking dryer, I wouldn't have to walk around naked!" I pulled a shirt out of the drawers and started to pull it on.

"I started it this morning before we left!" He turned and looked at me again to argue but his face turned red and he looked away again.

"Obviously, fucking not." I mumbled.

"What did you say-" he looked at me again,"Would you put on the damn shirt?!"

I stood there for a second, contemplating letting him suffer so I rolled my eyes and held the shirt in my hands,"I don't see the big deal. You were into me just a couple months ago."

He turned his back to me,"It's not that I'm not into you anymore-"

I walked up behind him slowly,"Then what is it?" I asked softly.

"You're overstepping." He shook his head.

I reached out from behind him and rested my hand on his side. "Then walk out." I whispered and moved my hand up to his shoulder. I had been dying to feel and rub his shoulders for months now.

He released a deep breath,"Come on. Knock it off."

I let my hand fall down to his hip then onto the side of his thigh when I pressed myself to his back.

He stepped forward quickly. "For fucks sakes, Mary." Then he headed towards the bathroom.

I giggled and slipped the shirt on. "Have a nice shower!"

Again it was just escalating more and more. I would purposely turn the dryer off right before we left in the mornings, so I wouldn't have dry towels. It benefited in two ways: One, I got to keep embarrassing Rip and Two, I got to bitch about the dryer which pissed him off because he swore he started the dryer before we left. Which he did.

One day it was after dark before we finished. I trudged up to the cabin with sore muscles. I was covered in dirt and mud and cow shit. I didn't want to drag it all through the cabin so I stripped down to my bra and panties on the porch, thinking Rip was over at dads house.

But I opened the door and sure enough Rip stood in the kitchen, drinking a beer. I froze like a deer in head lights. His face turned red and his eyes were wide.

"I- I didn't wanna get the house dirty-" I gestured to my clothes outside. "I thought you weren't here." I chuckled.

He dropped his head and tried to stifle back a laugh but failed. "You want a beer?" He asked and turned to the fridge to grab me one, knowing I never turned in down.

I stood there half naked, with my mouth gapped open. Is this payback? Is he trying to embarrass me now? I started this mess and I will finish it.

"Yeah, I do." I said softly.

He smiled,"I'm surprised." And he handed me the beer.

"You know I never turn down a beer." I twisted off the cap and took a long drink.

He nodded and just watched me. He was more confident than usual and it made him much hotter than normal. We stood in silence for a while.

We talked about what needed to be done this week before the new horses were dropped off. But I was starting to get cold.

"You cold?" He put his hand to my arm, only causing even more goose-bumps to appear.

"A little." I nodded.

"Let me turn the heat up."

The thermostat happened to be right above my head. He leaned in closer to me and reached up to mess with it. I took a sip of my beer and sat it in the corner. Preparing for what was about to happen. I reached out and rested my hand on his side.

"You might not wanna turn that up too much. You're kinda warm." I felt the heat radiating from him. I wanted to press myself against him and warm up that way.

"It is kinda warm already." He teased.

I grabbed the top of his jacket and pulled it down. He held slid it off. "Maybe if you took some clothes off it would help..." I whispered.

He left his hand by the thermostat and used it to prop himself up. He leaned into me more, almost pinning me to the wall. "Think so?" He whispered with a raspy voice. He rest his other hand on my hip and held me to the wall.

"Yes sir." I emphasized the sir, knowing what he told me before.

"Mmm. You don't make things easy, do you?" He used his thumb and ran it along the waist band of my panties. I thought I would fall over right then.

Suddenly the door flung open. Rip grabbed his jacket and held it over me. I grabbed it immediately as Lloyd turned the corner.

He froze. "I don't even wanna fucking know."

"What the hell, Lloyd?!" Rip started to walk towards him.

"They're here." He swallowed hard.

Rip turned and looked at me. "Don't leave." He pointed at me.

"Rip-"

"Do you understand me?" He raised his voice. "I don't want you out there."

"I can handle it." I said quietly. "I won't have a flash back. I can control it. Let me go with-" I started to ramble.

He shook his head,"Thats not why I don't want you going-"

"Then why?!" I hugged his jacket to my body tighter. Almost forgetting I didn't have any clothes on. "Im apart of this ranch too! I have the fucking brand!" I moved his jacket down.

Lloyd quickly looked at the ground and walked outside.

Rip paced around,"I don't have time to argue with you. Put on some fucking clothes and grab your gun." He stormed outside.

I ran to the bedroom and pulled on whatever I could find. Then I grabbed my M16 and an extra couple of clips. I shoved them in my coat pocket, jumped onto my boots, and grabbed my pistol that was sitting by the door. I shoved it behind my back and made my way fo the bunkhouse, quickly.

All the boys were gathered outside the door with their horses near by. I jogged up quietly.

They all jumped when I spoke up,"What's the plan?"

Jimmy cursed,"Fuck, Mary!"

Ryan put a hand to his chest,"You're like a fucking gazelle."

Adrenaline ran through my body. I felt like I was back overseas, getting ready for a mission. My legs aches and cramped to move and run.

Rip and Lloyd walked three horses out of the barn, and handed one off the me.

"They're at the new barn down by the creek. Last time the drone went by it looked like they're hiding out on the other side of the bank. There's only five that we can see." Lloyd explained as he mounted his horse.

The rest of us started to do the same.

"That side of the creek isn't ours, don't shoot 'em over there." Rip said.

Kasey rode down to us from the house,"Try not to shoot them at all. Just grab them first. See whys they're doing all this."

"Then shoot um." I finished.

Ryan chuckled.

Kasey sighed,"We'll see." He turned his horse towards Rip and trotted by. "We do this clean. I ain't covering up your stupid mistake again." I heard him mumble.

"That wasn't a mistake." Rip said back but louder.

Kasey stopped his horse. "Yeah but it was stupid."

I saw Rip take a deep breath in and his chest puffed out. I didn't have a clue what they were talking about but it was a sensitive topic. And Rip was pissed.

"You know-" He started in.

I lead my horse between them quickly,"Kasey, that's enough. We get your point. We'll do it by the book." I nodded at him.

Kasey stared around me at Rip then trotted off.

"You ain't been back long enough to know what the book is." Rip spat towards me.

"We're still doing that?" I asked. I grabbed my can of chew from my coat pocket and put a pinch in my lip. I saw his face turn red but he didn't have time to be pissed. We had to go.

"We'll talk when we get back." He huffed.

"Just talk?" I winked.

He looked at me sharply. He gave me a small scold but I swore I saw him holding back a smirk.

We all split up. Rip and Ryan were going to come up on them head on. Clint and Jimmy were going the long way around to meet them on the north and Colby, Lloyd, and I were the wall between them and the ranch on the south. If they got past us, they'd make it to the ranch before we could.

It wasn't a long ride. The new barn was only a few miles away. They were close.

It was a quiet night, no wolves or crickets or owls. And it was cold as always. I should've put on more layers. I took my hand off my gun and rubbed it on my leg to create some warmth. Colby looked over at me.

"Fucking cold." I whispered to him.

He chuckled quietly and shook his head. Then he pulled off his gloves and handed them to me.

"Are you sure?" I asked.

He nodded,"I'm fine. You're still not use to it yet."

I smiled and took them,"Thank you." I slipped them on. My hands warming up quickly especially from the heat that Colbys hands left in it. "Heard you gotcha girlfriend?" I teased.

He rolled his back eyes. "Hell fucking no."

"Not what I heard." I chuckled.

"Who told you that, Jimmy? Fucking Jimmy, I swear-" he started in.

Lloyd cut him off. "Would y'all shut the fuck up? You're gonna get us kill."

Colby stared at me as I stifled back a laugh.

About the time I looked back towards the creek, I saw Rip and Ryan trotted up to its banks. There was a little commotion then two men on horses stepped out from the other side.

"I thought you said 5?" I mumbled to Lloyd.

"That's what John said was on the drone." He quickly chimed back to me.

I rolled my eyes. "Great." When the fuck did we get drones.

Then we heard the running of horses. Within an instant nearly ten men and their horses approached the creek bank.

I pulled in my reins, ready to help but Lloyd stopped me.

"Let him call for us." Lloyd grabbed my reins.

"They're surrounded." I whispered yelled.

"You're not in charge here." He grumbled.

I breathed deeply, focusing back to Rip. My hands shook. I wanted to ride out there and stay beside him. I couldn't do anything this far away. I looked at Lloyd then out to Rip. Then back at Lloyd.

"He's okay." He said quietly and nodded. Reassuring me. I nodded a little but immediately looked out to him. I wanted to be with him. Help him.

But this is where he wanted me to be. And I have to except that because out here he's in charge. Im not on the front lines. Im bravo uniform.

Hell he didn't even want me here to start with.

It wasn't long before they crossed onto our land. Clint and Jimmy made their way towards them and sandwiched the outsiders between them and Rip.

The horses stirred. I couldn't take it any longer. It was about to be a stampede of pissed off horses. Someone was gonna get hurt.

"Lloyd, I think you better go help. It's about to get outta hand. We'll hang back." I sternly demanded.

"They can handle it-" he started it.

I turned to him,"Goddammit Lloyd, I'm not stupid. But that's double the men we were fucking expecting. Get out there, or I will."

He bit his tongue and looked out at them then back at me. "Your mouth is gonna get you in trouble one day." And he rode off.

"It already has." I mumbled and shook my head.

Three of the horses started to retreat back to the creek and one started braying and jumping back on his hind legs. The others started to stir but Lloyd was able to help herd them back.

"Good call." Colby whispered.

I nodded. Of course it was a good call. Anyone could've seen it coming.

We started there for a while longer just waiting. They must have been negotiating or arguing or who knows what.

"This is taking a long time." Colby mumbled.

"I know, it's worrying me." I tapped my finger on my rifle. "Got any binoculars?" I asked.

He shook his head,"Didn't even think about 'um."

"Fuck." I spit some tobacco juice out of my mouth and felt it burn my tongue. I hadn't chewed in a few weeks and my mouth wasn't use to it again.

"I'll be damned." Colby huffed.

"What?" I looked up. The horses were walking back over onto the other side of the creek. "We're letting them go?" Our boys starting riding back our way.

"Looks like it." He shook his head.

"No, they wouldn't agree to that." I tried to think hard. "Why would they wanna be out here anyway? That barn is empty."

Colby shrugged,"All that matters is they're out here and not at the ranch."

"Why wouldn't they go straight for the...for the ranch?" My mind started to spin.

The bunkhouse. The barns. The cabin. The house. Everything they could have wanted would be back at the ranch.

"You don't think..." His sentence trailed off. He was thinking what I was.

"We gotta go. Now." I turned my horse sharply and started to high tail it.

"Mary!" Colby called after me.

"They'll be right behind us!" I hollered back and kept going. He followed in close behind me.

We made it back at the ranch shortly after but stopped in the tree line. I saw a flash light in the barn.

"Get to the house. Make sure dad and Beth are okay." I ordered Colby. He nodded and started to move. "Hey."

He looked at me. Obviously nervous. "Yeah?"

"Don't let anyone near that fucking house. Yell for me if you need something."

"I will. Be careful." And then he took off.

I let out a deep breath and dismounted my horse. I walked her over to one of the corrals closer to the barn but not too close. I didn't want anyone to hear me. I switched the safety off my gun and started towards the barn.

I checked back at the tree line. The rest of the boys should be back soon. They weren't far behind us.

I looked through a window in the barn. Two men were rummaging through everything. Causing a huge mess.

I put my back to the wall. One had a pistol behind his back and I couldn't tell by the other. They wouldn't be expecting anyone though.

I slowly walked to the entrance. I released a breath and steadied my weapon to my shoulder. I turned the corner.

"Get on your fucking knees, don't make a sound." I said sharply. They both jumped. They never even heard me walk in.

On hit his knees and put his hands behind his head. The other one, the one I knew had a gun behind he back just stood with his hands out.

"I know you have a gun behind your back. Don't make me shoot you." I said quietly and calmly. He clenched his jaw then hit his knees. I glanced behind me quickly. "No one else in here?" I asked.

The scared one shook his head. The other one didn't say a word. I stepped behind his back and yanked out his gun then patted him down. And I patted the other one down.

I looked around quickly for something to tie them up with. I expect the boys to be back to help me. It worried me. Something must had happened.

I zip tied ones hands behind his back and then to his ankles. I did the same with the other and made them go into separate horse stalls. I locked the stalls then zip tied then as well. There was no way they were getting out.

I checked towards the bunk house. There was nothing there anyone would want and I saw no movement.

Then I looked up at Rips cabin. There was a light on in the bedroom. We didn't leave a light on in there. Only the kitchen and porch light.

I glanced at the tree line. Nothing. Then I looked at the cabin. It was a long ways from anything so if I needed help it would be a while for anyone to be there, if anyone even knew I was there or came back.

My army instincts were telling me no. Wait for back up.

But this isn't the army. This my home.

16

R ips cabin held a special place in my heart.

When growing up it was just a spare cabin on the ranch. All of us kids would go and play on the front porch and sometimes sneak in even when we weren't allowed it. I would walk up to it when I got in fights with Dad or my brothers and sit on the front porch steps, watching the world in front of it. It was peaceful and gave me a sense of freedom. I would let my imagination go and pretend it was my own cabin and I was drinking coffee on the front porch like an adult would. Or I was off work for the day and drinking a beer like I watched my father do.

Maybe it's special because it's my safe place now not just when I was a child and ran off to hide when I was upset or in trouble. It's where I go now when I'm feeling alone. And whether Rip is the person I want to be around or not, he was a person. And that's all I really needed to feel okay sometimes. I spent so much time alone in Afghanistan, that any person that spoke English and looked safe, was all I needed to feel better.

So when I saw someone creeping around in the cabin, I felt personally attacked. I spent so many years killing people in their own homestead that it was uncomfortable to see someone in mine. Not uncomfortable, it was pissing me off.

I pushed open the cabin door slowly. It didn't creak. Thank god it didn't, when it always does. Especially when I come in late from the bars and Rip is asleep on the couch.

I heard the person in the bedroom, throwing things around, rummaging through papers. What the hell were these people looking for?

I checked behind the door. Nothing. Nothing behind the island in the kitchen. I slowly started for the bedroom. I checked the bathroom quickly. Nothing.

I silently thanked my grandfather for building a cabin with such a simple layout.

I turned the corner to the bedroom. There stood a man, average height. Leather gloves, black cowboy boots, black jeans, dark green long sleeves and a leather black vest. A terrible sense in fashion obviously. He had a trunk that I had never seen before dumped onto the bed. He didn't hear me come in.

"Who the fuck are you?" I asked, my pistol drawn towards him.

He didn't jumped. He just stopped looking and turned his head to look at me.

"Does it matter? You're gonna kill me anyways." The man huffed. His hair was unkempt and long. A dirty brown color.

I shook my head,"I don't wanna shoot you. Just wanna know why y'all are here."

He sighed,"You don't wanna shoot someone? The infamous Mary Dutton, doesn't wanna kill. Isn't that your job?" He asked hatefully.

I swallowed hard. How does he know me. Who the fuck is this. "My job was to keep Afghan people safe against the Taliban. That was my job. Now who the hell are you and what do you want?" I spoke up.

He shook his head. "To keep them safe, huh? That didn't go well, right?"

I let out a small breath. Trying to keep myself calm. I knew his was trying to get under my skin. I just didn't know why.

"Is there a fucking point you wanna make? Yeah our government is fucked up and pulled out troops too soon. And a bunch of people we tried to protect lost their lives. Now who the fuck are you?!" I yelled and pointed my pistol harshly at him. Keeping calm was apparently out of the question now.

He chuckled. "That's the Mary I remember. You don't remember me?" I tried to think hard. I shook my head. There was no one. "Ah, how sad. Your father definitely remembers me. And what he stole from me!" The man yelled.

I was shocked. But even more shocked when I felt my knee being kicked in from the back.

"Ah!" I yelled in pain but turned quickly. A flash of a people stood behind me. I swung my pistol and hit the person in the head.

They returned a punch to my face. I glanced to check the other man but he was out of my sight. A new man came running down the hall way, weapon drawn. Without thinking, I aimed my pistol and shot a few rounds while the man I was fighting grabbed my head and threw me into the picture frame hanging up. I watched the hallway man fall back. I tackled the man treating me like a rag doll and knocked him onto his back. I lifted his shoulder and smashed his head onto the ground. He fought to roll over onto me and won. He was much bigger and heavier than me. I didn't want to shoot another person but I was going to lose this fight.

He wrapped his hands around my neck and squeezed. I reached by my leg to grab a knife but realized I wasn't in combat. I didn't have my gear on. I didn't have back up in the way. I was alone and I had to live. I couldn't let Rip walk into his own cabin and see me laying dead on the floor because I gave up a fight.

I reached in my coat pocket and grabbed the clip for my M16 and slammed it into the mans head. He groaned and fell sideways. I grabbed my pistol and aimed it to him. I started to squeeze the trigger but stopped.

"Please. I don't wanna kill anymore people." I beg the man, blood pooling in the corners of my mouth.

He put his hands up. I breathed heavily and glanced around me. Just then I heard someone yelling.

"Mary!" Then someone running onto the porch. It was Rip.

"I'm okay!" I yelled back as he turned the corner and looked down the hallway. First at the dead man laying in his floor. Then at the man I was holding at gun point. Then at me. His eyes were full of worry. He looked worse than I assumed I looked. A busted eyebrow and bloody mouth. Blood pooling from his hands and down the front of his jeans. It was a blood bath.

"Rip, what happened?" My voice cracked.

17

He helped me tie up the man and had Ryan and Lloyd guard him. They looked awful too.

Luckily no one made it to the house yet.

Rip walked me onto the porch.

"Are you okay?" He held my face with both hands. Inspecting every part of my face.

I stepped back and brushed his hands away. "Seriously, I'm fine. This is nothing new for me." I sighed. "Now what the hell happened out there?"

He clenched his jaw and just stared at me. I couldn't tell if he was pissed or upset or worried. Or maybe just trying to process everything. I did just shoot a man in his house. He cleared his throat, "Uh Jimmy saw y'all take off and he tried to follow. They realized you were on to them and they started in on us."

I opened my mouth to talk but couldn't find any words. "You need to be checked out. That head wound looks bad." Was all I could say.

He nodded slowly. "Come on." And he started to walk down to the barn. I followed.

"I think one guy got away. He said my father stole something from him and that's what their looking for." I said as we walked down the hill. I saw cop cars and ambulances around the barn. It was a strange sight to see.

"Make sure you tell the sheriff." Rip patted my back.

"Since when do we actually follow protocol and not just say we did?" I chuckled.

"Since Kasey became Livestock Commissioner." He grumbled.

We made it to the barn and I forced Rip to see a paramedic.

Then I saw Kasey. He walked over to me and hugged me.

"It was a clean shot. They're not even gonna investigate it." He mumbled under his breath to me. I nodded. Good. That was the last thing I needed.

I let the medics look at me. No stitches or anything needed. Just lots of bruises and bangs.

"I ain't going to a fucking hospital." I heard Rip argue behind me.

I thanked the medic and jogged towards him and the paramedic he was with.

"What's going on?" I rested my hand on Rips shoulder and pushed him gently to sit back down onto the ambulance. He did so.

"He wants me to go to the fucking hospital-" Rip started in.

"Why, what's wrong?" I asked the paramedic.

He sighed,"With this deep of a head wound, he needs blazing and a CT to check for concussions or hemorrhaging."

I looked down at Rip then back at the paramedic. "Look, he's not gonna go. And if he does have a concussion, it's not the first brain damage he's suffered from. If there's a hemorrhage he'll die before y'all get there. We've a shit ton of yarrow powder that works better than any blazing. Can you use that?" I asked.

The medic sighed again,"It's really not sanitary-"

I giggled a little and blinked up at the medic,"Trust me, this place is cleaner than any hospital. Come on, he's going to refuse treatment no matter what. Just make it quick and easy."

The medic smiled and rolled his eyes. "Alright, fine. Where's the powder?"

I walked over to the cabinets and grabbed a bottle of wonder dust and handed it to the medic.

"Better thank your wife, buddy." The medic chuckled.

My face turned red.

"Not my fucking wife." Rip grumbled.

"Sorry, girlfriend." The medic sprayed a little of the powder on his wound then brushed it off. The bleeding stopped almost immediately.

"Nope, just a pain in the ass."

I chuckled.

"Ah okay, apologizes." The medic finished cleaning up his wound and butterfly bandaged it together after gluing it. When he was finished he looked up at me just flirty eyes. "So you're single? That's good to know."

I giggled.

Rip stood up immediately and pointed away from us. "Get the fuck outta here if you don't wanna end up in the coroners van too."

The medic clumsily gathered his things and stumbled off.

"Necessary?" I asked.

Rip looked down at me. I was relieved for us all to be alive and standing. I wasn't happy but I wasn't mad. I was okay. We had three live people that I knew of to investigate and that was a start. But he was pissed.

"Definitely necessary. He was looking at you like-"

"Like I'm pretty?" I cut him off. He blinked blankly. I caught him off guard. "Because even if you don't see it, I am. And it got you out of going to the hospital and saved you thousands of dollars in medical bills and from being anyway from the ranch tonight." I rolled my eyes and started walking over to everyone else.

They all looked rough. I still didn't know what happened out there. And it was the last thing I wanted to talk about. I was just glad they're all alive.

Jimmy was sitting in a milk crate, letting the medic I had clean his hands.

"You doing okay?" I asked quietly. He looked up at me with worrisome eyes. He was still in shock. It was the look Jake gave me on his first mission out.

"It was- they were...there was a lot of blood." He whispered.

I squeezed his shoulder, "It's okay. It's over now. It's done." He nodded. "We'll talk when you feel like talking." I rubbed his back for a moment then walked over to Ryan and Colby.

"I should've went with you." Colby blurted out.

I shook my head,"No. You needed to protect the house. That's where they were headed next."

"Mary."

I turned to see my dad walking into the barn. Nearly jogging.

"Dad." I walked towards him. Surprisingly he grabbed me and wrapped his arms around me. I didn't care how mad I was for him kicking me out. All I wanted was my dad. I hugged him back tightly. "I'm okay, dad." I whispered.

He let you go and grabbed my face. He inspected it. "Good, good. If you need time to heal-"

"Really, I'm fine." I insisted and brushed his hands away just like I did Rip earlier.

"Okay." He cleared his throat. "Okay. Well I'm gonna talk to Kasey about what happened." He took a couple steps then stopped. "Mary, if you need to stay at the house for a while, I- it's fine." He said it all very quietly and somberly.

I nodded. "I'm happy where I'm at, Dad. But thanks." He huffed again and walked on to Kasey. "Wait-" He turned to look at me. A thousand questions ran through my head. Who the fuck are these guys? Who the fuck was THAT guy? What do they want from us? This isn't just about the airport. There's no way. But I didn't ask anything. "I love you." Is what came out.

"I love you too, kid."

Then he went along his way.

18

We walked into Rips cabin early that morning. Maybe 3am. The sheriffs department had taken a few things. The big one was the rug that was soaked in the guys blood I shot. I walked over to it. The rug was gone but blood had soaked through it and stained the hard wood floor.

"I'll see what I can do to get that out-" I turned to tell Rip but he was already grabbing the rug from the kitchen. He threw it on top of the drain with a loud plop.

"I don't wanna think about that every time I walk by." He grumbled and walked on to the bathroom. I heard the shower turn on.

I was left standing alone in the middle of the cabin where I had just shot a man, beat the hell out of a man, and almost died. I looked around. Everything looked normal until you got to the bed room. It was trashed.

I grabbed the chest off the bed and started putting papers back into it. I didn't even take the time to be nosey and read them.

Rip stepped out of the shower shortly after, just with a towel around his waist. I looked at him momentarily before realizing I was staring. My face turned red as he walked over to grab his clothes. As if this was something new and I didn't both him all the time with it.

I had taken a shower in the bunkhouse earlier while waiting to be able to come back to the cabin so I just changed clothes. I finally got most things cleaned up in the bedroom. And although I've been the one sleeping in the bed, it felt wrong this time. I didn't wanna be in there. Alone.

I walked into the living room quietly. Rip laid on the couch, facing the door with his pistol on the night stand.

I waited for him to say something but he didn't. So I sat down in the chair beside the couch. I pulled my knees up to my chest and hugged them. I rested my face on my knees. Rips eyes stared wide open at the door.

"You are." His tired, raspy voice sounded weak.

"What?" I asked, confused.

He looked at me,"Pretty." Was all he said. My heart skipped a little beat. A smile pulled on my lips. It had been a long time since anyone had called me anything like that. "Better get some rest. We're breaking horses tomorrow."

I looked down the hallway were I shot a guy only hours before.

The good thing about Afghanistan was you never saw the same place once. Maybe we were there for 48 hours straight but we never went back to where we killed someone. And here I had to look it straight in the face.

"That guy... he said Dad stole something from him." I mumbled.

Rip cleared his throat,"Mary... you know I think a lot of your father," He turned to look at me,"But he's taken a lot of things from a lot of people."

The words sent chills down my spine. I already knew but never let myself get too far into it. I nodded slowly,"This felt different. This can't be about the land-"

"People want ground. They want land. And they'll done stupid shit to get it." He kept turning me down and not listening.

I sighed loudly and rolled my eyes.

"Come on, now, don't pout about it." He turned his head but to the door.

"I am not pouting." I furrowed my eyebrows and leaned forward in my chair, pissed at what he said.

Then he chuckled and glanced at me.

I huffed and leaned back with a thump. I glanced back down the hallway.

"You not going to bed?" He asked quietly.

"I don't know if I can." I whispered back.

He turned to me again. But with a different look. "We're gonna find out who's doing this. And we'll find that fucking guy. I'll make sure of it."

I swallowed hard.

Then Rip got up from the couch slowly. He stood in front of me and reached his hand out. "Let's go to bed." My chest tightened and my stomach flipped and flopped. I stared at his hand then up at him. "I'll take you back there. Come on."

I put my hand in his and stood up. He squeezed my hand and walked me back to the bedroom. I stopped at the door way where I stopped hours before.

"This was suppose to be where I felt safe." A tear slipped from my face. I quickly brushed it away, realizing I probably wasn't even upset, just fussy like a baby who hadn't slept or ate in hours.

Rip gave me a small, sad smile. He put his hand behind my back and helped me walk forward. Something that almost felt impossible to do. He pulled back the covers on the bed and let me lay down. I rolled onto my side and curled into a ball, just completely weak and drained and alone.

And I thought he had left because I heard the light switch flip off and it got dark. I left out a small sighed.

I told myself when I left Afghanistan I would never hurt another person. And that's all I've done since I've been home.

I felt the other side of the bed get heavy and saw Rip lay down beside me. "Come here." He whispered.

I stared at him. Not knowing what to do, I swallowed hard. I wanted to but part of me still hated him. Hated how he was a different man every hour. And hated how he treated me at times. Like I didn't know what I was doing and as if I couldn't do certain things.

But for once, I did what he said. I moved in close to his body. He opened his arms and I fell in beside him. I laid my hands and head on his chest and sighed. He dropped his arms around me. "I'm sorry." He whispered and kissed the top of my head. "I should've known this was going to happen."

I didn't say anything back. I wanted to ask how he would've known but I was scared for the answer.

Within minutes the sound of the front door opening filled my ears. We both jumped out of bed. I grabbed my M16 and I saw him start to head to the door. But I tightly wrapped my finger on the trigger, ready to blow to bits anyone that barged in. Suddenly an older man came in through the threshold and was yelling. Coming towards me. I stepped forward and yelled back at him.

"Get on the fucking ground!" I yelled, ready to shoot. But Rip was coming towards me. The man looked stunned and put his hands up.

"Hey, hey, hey! Mary, it's your dad. It's John." Rip put himself between my gun the man.

I lowered my rifle and Rip slowly moved.

Sure enough, my father was there, breathing deeply and anxiously. Suddenly any worry I had about an intruder left my mind and I was terrified of other things. Like the fact my father just found Rip and I together.

"What the fuck is going here?" Dad looked Rip up and down. "That's my daughter!" His face turned red.

"Sir-" Rip lowered his voice.

"Dad- it's my fault-" I spoke up.

"No, it's not." Rip shook his head,"I told her-"

"Rip, don't-" I tossed my rifle on the bed.

He clenched his jaw and now his face was turning red too,"Goddammit, Mary, that's enough. Keep your mouth shut or get out."

My eyes were wide then my breath caught in my throat.

Dad threw his hands in the air,"All I need is someone sitting guard at the fucking barn. And I find this. Someone tell me what in the hell is going on and it better be a good goddamn answer."

Rip released a deep breath,"When we hired Keith back, I told Mary she had to stay somewhere else."

Dad stared down at me, then back at Rip. Then back at me. I felt like a teenage girl who snuck her boyfriend into the house and we got caught.

Dad put his hands on his hips and turned around. Then he started to pace. I started to expect the worst. I ran thousands of scenarios in my head.

If he kicked me out of the ranch completely, I could stay at the Res with Monica. Or maybe Jamie would help me. If anything I can stay at the motel in town for a few days until he calms down.

I could go with John.

I glanced over at my phone. I could call him. He'd be here within the next 24 hours.

"I told you," Dad pointed his finger at Rip,"That you treat her, like she's a wrangler. That's all you had to fucking do."

Rip nodded but turned into shaking his head. "Sir, when I started here, my job was to keep her and Beth safe. That's what I'm trying to do."

Dad threw his hands up again,"Keith wasn't going to do anything!"

"How do you know that?!" I yelled. It was my turn to talk.

"Mary, stay out of this-" Rip looked at me with sad eyes.

"No! You people wonder why I left this place! Because everyone's so worried about control and putting on a show for everyone else to see. I mean, why do you people think this whole goddamn mess happened tonight?! Because we give them a reason to do this! But I don't want to be in this. I just wanna work cattle. So if this is really a problem, if this,"I let out a deep breath and closed my eyes briefly,"I'll stay in that bunkhouse. But if you wake up next week, and he's no where to be found." I shook my head and chuckled a small, sarcastic chuckle,"Don't be surprised if you never find him." I grabbed my gun and my bag in the corner. And out the door I went.

"Mary-" I heard Rip try to follow but then I heard my dad start yelling again.

I pushed my feet forward and trudged through the pasture and down the hill. My mind was racing.

Do I call John? I could leave with him and never have to worry about this place. But my heart stung for Rip. Remembering what Lloyd told me about how he acted when I was gone. And I didn't wanna leave Colby and Ryan and Jimmy.

Soon I was in front of the bunkhouse doors. I sighed. There was noise inside but not happy and upbeat like normal. I grabbed the door handle and made my way in. Jimmy's eyes met mine. He was sitting at the table, cleaning a rifle. He glanced at my bag. Then back at me. Worry obviously filled his eyes.

I heard a chuckle from the corner. It was Keith.

I walked to my old bunk and threw my bag onto it. Then I pulled a knife out of it and marched straight over to him.

"Mary-" Ryan hollered. "Come on, there's been enough blood for the night."

I was within a foot of Keith when I stopped. I craved to make him as uncomfortable as he use to make me.

"You look at me,"I took a deep breath in and stared down at him sitting on his bunk in the corner,"You talk to me, you even think about me and I will cut out your fucking tongue, old man. I killed over 100 towel heads so don't think I'll won't bat an eye to take your life. You hear me?" I spoke slow and deep. I meant every word. He stared up at me. I'm sure he wasn't scared but he knew I was serious.

I questioned even waiting. I couldn't cut his throat here and now.

He gave a small nod and I turned around. I tried hard to let out of breath as quietly as possible but it felt so heavy and strained.

I tried to sleep that night but couldn't. I laid awake, listening for foot steps in the hardwood floor. From Keith or the other people coming back. But I never heard them. All I heard was Jimmy rolling back and forth, never sleeping either.

"Jimmy, get some rest." I whispered softly to him.

"I don't know how you do it. I can't get any of it out of my head." He sighed.

I didn't say anything back. There was nothing I could say to help and fix it.

The next few weeks were full of breaking horses. Something I use to love but haven't got to do in years.

There were no leads on the people that attacked and robbed us. They took eight guys into custody but all eight had either escaped, disappeared or been murdered.

I also hadn't seen Rip very often. Dad made sure to have our schedules misaligning. Kasey took over Rips position and Rip was... I really don't know where. But he was always with Dad and Beth when going to meeting and conferences. It's doubtful that's by choice. I'm sure he was dying to get back to the cattle but he had to play out the punishment my father was giving him for "sleeping" with his daughter.

I didn't really miss him. Maybe I should. But I was able to go out to the bars whenever and not be questioned or side eyed for staying out too late or drinking too much. And I enjoyed being with the boys in the bunkhouse again, minus Keith. We all played poker and drank and watched football together. We'd go to rodeos together on the weekends again. It was nice to be back.

"Cowboy, you try and break that youngun, first." Clint was separating us all into different pens. Jimmy, Colby, Ryan and I had the younger ones.

I jumped in the little arena and tightened on a saddle. I was sore and hurting for the combat I had from weeks before, but there was work to be done.

The horse was fine with the saddle and bit. I put my left foot into the stirrups. He started to stir. Great. I mentally rolled my eyes. Getting on him wasn't going to be fun. I let out a deep breath and grabbed the top of his saddle. Then I tried to pull myself up.

He took off like a bullet. My left foot was in but I didn't even have time to swing my right leg over. The horse rammed himself into the side of the pen. He sandwiched me between the panels and himself. I grunted and let go of the saddle, then hit the ground with a thump.

I sighed and stood up slowly.

"Ya alright?" Colby hollered. I spit a wad of tobacco juice onto the ground. It was also easier to chew since I wasn't living with Rip. I nodded to Colby and wanted back to the pain in the ass of a horse.

I tried to get on multiple times but he just kept throwing me. I didn't mind. It was motivation to do something. Fix something. I needed the beating. It would put my head back on straight. Get everything out of head. Mostly Rip. I felt my whole body aching but hell it was nice to finally feel something again.

"She sure looks good riding don't she?" I heard someone say when they walked by.

I snapped my head over. Sure enough, Keith was there watching.

My heart started racing. I was pissed, ready to get rid of him.

But I calmed myself and told myself I would break this horse. And I did within a few hours.

I walked the horse out of the arena and into the stables.

"You get him broke?" Rip was in the barn.

"Yes sir." I said, out of habit. I immediately stopped when I realized who was speaking to me. I jerked my head up and looked up at him, a small smile breaking through my lips.

"Get your ass out of here." He said harshly but definitely teasing.

I chuckled and walked on to the stalls. I walked the horse into the stalls then rubbed his head and nose. When I walked out, Rip was still there.

He cleared his throat,"It was strange not having someone else at the cabin lately." He spoke softly.

I nodded and looked down at my dirt covered self, reminding me of the last time I walked into his cabin nearly naked, to avoid getting things dirty. The day everything happened. "Yeah, haven't seen ya in a while." I whispered.

He nodded. "I know. I'm sorry." I looked into his eyes. He meant it. It wasn't very often Rip apologized so I knew he was serious. He took the toothpick from between his teeth out. "How about you come up tonight for dinner?" He asked.

I was hesitant, knowing where this could lead to again. But maybe I had missed staying with Rip honestly. And I was realizing that now. "Yeah, I will."

"Good." He winked then walked out.

I smiled and looked down at my feet.

"Shoo that looks good." I heard the disgusting voice again.

I swallowed hard and started to walk out. But he grabbed my arm.

"Get your fucking hands off of me." I gritted my teeth.

His dark green eyes stared darkly at me. And he tightened his grip on my arm. "You're gonna do what I tell you." He grumbled and reached between my legs.

I swung my leg arm and hit him square in the nose. He grunted but didn't let go. He shoved me up into a stall door and tried shoving his hand up my layers of shirts. I started kicking and fighting but he had a tight grip.

"I'm gonna get what I tried to get years ago." He whispered in my ear then let go of me all together.

He took a few steps back and stared at me while walking away. When he was out of my sight, I hit my knee. Then I sat back against the door and hugged my knees.

I tried hard not to cry but I couldn't help it. A few tears fell and a gasp escaped my mouth. I sniffled. Then I stopped. And decided it was time.

Time to make a plan.

We all worked until late that night. 9 o'clock everyone was packing up. Keith was the last in the barn to put up his saddle. He always was. I stayed in a stall and watched through the bars.

I glanced out the window. Ryan closed the door to the bunkhouse. No one else was out here besides me and Keith. I pulled my pistol out from behind my back and slowly walked up to Keith. I pushed the barrel into his back and he jumped, then tried to turn around.

"I'll fucking kill you. Now walk." I grumbled.

He listened.

And I walked him out into the woods. Deep into the woods. Where the coyotes would find him eventually and take care of the mess I was about to make.

He didn't say but a few words. He knew the promise I had made a few weeks ago. And I was going to keep it.

"Get on your fucking knees." I huffed and shoved him toward the ground. He did so. "You know," I sighed and pulled out my old hunting knife we used for moose. It was sharp and painful,"If you would've never showed up here again, you could've lived. But you came back."

He looked up at me as he got down on both knees. "But then I'd never get to feel that soft skin of yours again-"

I gritted my teeth as I swung the knife across his neck.

He feel backwards and started gurgling, trying to talking. But couldn't. He was still alive.

I shook my head. I could let him bleed out in peace.

Or in pain. I pushed open his mouth and grabbed his tongue then cut that off. His eyes opened wide and the gurgles got louder and he tried to scream but choke on his own blood.

I smirked and leaned over him,"You can thank the hajis for that. They taught me that one."

I turned around and started walking back to the ranch. I decided to wash off in the barn. I turned on the faucet and washed my hands off, along with Keith's tongue. I grabbed a rag off of the closet and wrapped it in it. There was blood on my sweatshirt so I pulled it off and tossed it in a metal barrel, along with the handle of the knife. It was plastic and it would metal. I tossed the blade into the scrape bin of metal to be melted.

I took my cigarette lighter and lit the sweatshirt, then tossed it in the trash can. The fire got a little bigger but it wouldn't burn for long. I walked in to the bunkhouse and everyone stared me way.

"Mary." Lloyd whispered.

"Hm?" I tossed the rag onto the table and kept walking. I pulled off my tshirt and long sleeve shirt.

Colby reached onto the table and grabbed the rag. "What the fuck?!" He tossed it back on the table.

"What?" Jimmy popped up from the couch and everyone stood around the table.

I turned around from everyone and I clipped my bra, just to put on a black lace one. Then I slipped a quarter zip Sherpa on top of it.

"Mary..." Jimmy shook his head. Then everyone was silent.

"What? I warned him." I pushed my jeans down and slipped into clean ones.

Everyone stared at me and I put my cowboy hat on the rack and fluffed my hair. I ran a quick comb through it then slipped in my boots.

"Be back later." And I was out of the door.

"Hang on." Lloyd followed.

"What, now? You act like this is something new, that we never do-" I walked backwards a few steps and threw my hands in the air.

Lloyd nodded,"Do you need any help?" He grumbled.

I paused. He was on my side. I shook my head,"The coyotes will get the rest."

He looked at the ground and cleared his throat. "Alright." Then he walked off.

I shook my head and headed up to Rips cabin. I smiled at the stepped on the porch and could hear him snoring from outside. Something I had actually missed a little. I released a deep breath and debated with myself. I either go inside and act like I didn't hear him asleep or I go back down to the bunkhouse.

I really don't want him to think I didn't show up. So I pushed down on the door handle and stepped in. He still snored. I chuckled a little and slipped off my boots. I walked over and sat in the little chair I always found the most comfortable. I propped my feet up on the table and stared at the fire as I drank my beer. I enjoyed the safe feeling I rarely had. But I had just killed a man that was making me feel extremely unsafe and now I was with a man who made be feel like I always safe with him.

I sighed. John made me feel safe but only when he was around. And he wouldn't understand why I killed Keith. He wouldn't be okay with killing just to get rid of people. He was more ethical and probably innocent other than what the military had him do. But Rip would understand. Maybe. He wouldn't be happy about me doing it myself. If he knew, he would scold me for not telling him and letting him handle it. All in all, the less both of them knew the better.

Rip kept sawing logs but I was getting hungry. I hadn't ate anything since breakfast this morning. I stood up and walked to the kitchen and decided to fix a cowboy casserole. I knew Rip would have everything for it. He kept the supplies in hand because it was his favorite thing I made. A pound of ground beef and a pound of spicy ground sausage with onions and jalapeños then mix in with baked beans and poured into a casserole dish. A box of jiffy corn bread with a bunch of honey and pour that on top of the beans and beef mixture. Then bake it. It was quick to throw together and thankfully fairly quiet. He tossed and turned a couple turns but never fully woke up. I opened myself another beer.

The snoring stopped and he slowly sat up and looked in my direction.

"I just fixed dinner and you barely budged. But I open one beer..." I shook my head and tossed my hands up.

He chuckled and got up from the couch. He hadn't even changed from working earlier. And I didn't mind. He pulled his jacket off, revealing just a black tshirt. One of the many shirts I bought a few months ago for him. I caught myself staring at his shoulders and arms but stopped before he noticed.

He walked to the fridge and grabbed himself a beer. "Whatcha fix?" He took a long drink.

I smiled,"Take a guess."

He paused and his eyes lit up,"Did you really?" He opened the oven.

I laughed and smiled even wider.

"Damn." He smiled back at me. And for once things seemed simple. And easy. And happy.

His tshirt hung off his chest a little. "Did those shirts stretch in the wash?" I smoothed the cloth to his chest with my hand.

He took another long drink,"No, you ain't around cooking every night so I've dropped a few pounds." He chuckled.

I rolled my eyes and sat down at the bar stools. "I cook at the bunkhouse every night. You know you can come down there and eat."

He nodded,"yeah okay." Then we just stared at one another. "How are things down there?" It came out as a whisper.

I nodded,"As expected. Just how it is." I shrugged and took a swing of the beer then sat it down.

He cleared his throat and leaned on the counter in between us. "I know. But I rather you be here with me."

I didn't know what to say and how to take it. Thankfully I was saved by the timer buzzing. I grabbed a pot holder and pulled it out, looked at it, then decided to put it back in. Just a few more minutes.

I reached over to grab my beer. He snatched it up off the counter with a shit eating grin on his face.

I giggled and shook my head. He took a drink out of it then started to hand it back. I reached out and he moved it back.

"Come on." I laughed a little more and stepped towards it.

He put the bottle to his lips,"I don't know, I'm kinda thirsty." He drank more of it. I just smiled at him. Weeks ago I would've fought him for it or actually have gotten pissed that he was picking on me. But all I could do was smile. I was truly happy. "What's that look about?" He sat the beer down between us. He almost squinted his eyes to see me better.

I shrugged,"Just happy to be here."

He smirked a little and huffed,"I ain't ever heard that come out of your mouth."

I glanced at his lips. "You ain't heard a lot of things come out of my mouth." I said quietly. His smirked faded and I watched his chest rise and fall.

He took a step closer to me, slowly. I just watched him.

He reached out and put his rough, calloused hand on the side of the neck and brought it up to hold my face. He closed the space between us. I rested my hands on his side. "You know, we should probably talk about all this before we do anything. I don't know if we want the same things." I whispered up at him.

"I don't fucking care. I want you. And I've wanted you for a long time. Just let me have it for tonight and you can break my heart after." He teased and a smiled grew on my lips.

"That's the plan." I stretched up and pressed my lips to his jaw and kissed softly.

"Goddammit, Mary." He let out a breath. I moved my lips to his neck and ran my hand up to his chest. I loved how tight and broad his chest was. How manly his felt. I wanted to engulf me into his arms. He turned his head down to me and rested his forehead on mine. Both of us breathing heavy. "Are you sure you wanna do this? I don't want you to feel like you have too." He whispered.

I closed my eyes. "I really want this. I need this, Rip." I opened my eyes and stared deep into his. He pressed his lips onto mine. I melted into him and wrapped my arms around his neck. He did the same to my waist and picked me up off the ground. I pulled my legs up and wrapped them around him. Soon we were in the bedroom. I never kissed someone so hard and so deep before. I couldn't get enough. I was so overwhelmed with emotion I could either cry or scream. He laid me down on the bed and I quickly pulled my sweatshirt off. He leaned back down to kiss me and started kissing my neck deeply. I let a moan escape my mouth.

"Mmm, that's the prettiest thing I've ever heard." He planted soft kisses around my ear.

Tears formed in my eyes but I blinked them away. I wasn't going to cry when we were about to have sex. What in the hell is wrong with me? But a tear escaped my eye and ran down the side of my face.

He stopped immediately. "What's wrong, darling?" He was hovering over me.

I shook my head,"Nothing. I just..." I pushed out a deep breath,"I... You make me feel safe and... like I'm..." I lost my words.

He pushed my hair back out of my face. "Like you're beautiful?" I nodded. "Because you are. And I hope you never forget that." He started kissing my neck again. "Just relax, honey."He said softly.

Darling. Honey. They both made me feel some type of way.

Say it again please. Don't ever stop saying it.

I let out another breath and did as I was told. It felt amazing and I let another moan leave my lips. "Mmmm." My eyes slowly shut. He kissed down to my collarbone and to my chest which set a fire off into my stomach. I grabbed his face and brought it back to my lips. And we kept kissing for what could've been hours but felt like minutes. Like two teenagers who were making out for the first time.

Soon the hardcore make out turned into soft kisses and just being wrapped up into each other's arms. He kissed my lips softly again and then kissed my forehead. I rested my face into his chest and sighed. I was tired and we hadn't even had sex. God, I'm getting old.

He tightened his grip on me and opened his mouth to speak. But he was cut off by a loud beeping siren.

"Fuck." I jumped up and ran into the kitchen. I heard him slowly follow behind. Black smoke barreled from the stove. "Oh hell." I grabbed potholders and opened the oven door. Smoke rolled out. I squinted as my eyes burned from the heat. I reached in and grabbed the casserole dish, but my hand slipped forward and I cursed as I felt my finger tips grazed the hot glass pan. They burned and surely blistered. I sat the pan on the counter and pulled up the door closed. "Damnit." I threw the pot holders down harshly on the counter as well and flicked on the cold water faucet. I put my hand under it and let the cold water take the heat from my finger tips.

"Ya okay?" Rip rested his hand on my lower back.

I nodded,"Yeah, my hand just slipped." I glanced at the casserole pan. Which was filled with blackened cornbread and baked beans. The pan was even black and probably would've shattered and caught fire it the alarms hadn't gone off. "Sorry about dinner."

He chuckled and shook his head,"It's okay. I'm not too worried about it."

I turned the water off and looked at my hand. Surely enough, two of my fingers were red and already had the flesh bubbling up.

I inhaled deeply to sigh. But froze.

The burnt flesh smell filled my nose. I blinked. And I was gone.

19

"Corporal." My radio buzzed. "This is November echo delta flying in. We can pick up wounded."

It was staticky and cutting out. I shot my eyes to Jake. He shook his head.

"Not me. No. You put other people on that chopper." He was leaned against a beaten and battered wall. We finally made it back inside the building. He was propped up with his backpack but he looked terrible. He was pale skinned though the dirt in his face.

"That's not your decision." I grabbed my rifle and stood up. I called back to NED and set locations for a pick up. I reached down to grab Jake.

"No." He spoke up but wouldn't move. "I'll get the next one. Let the other guys go first. They gotta get outta here."

I swallowed hard. "Jake," I squatted down to him, "You have to get home too."

"And I will. But not yet. Let them go first. Corporal," His voice started to shake. "I'm not done here yet."

I stood up and nudged his leg with my foot. He winced. "You can't even walk." I clenched my jaw. "You're not any help here."

I watched him swallow hard. And his face turn red. And he sat up. Wincing, and groaned, he stood up. Grabbed his rifle. "I'm not leaving. I'm covering you while you get them to the loading zone. Let's go."

I stared up at him and a smiled formed on my face, I patted his arm. "Lead the way, private."

I figured if we were both gonna die here, which we most likely were, it was best to let him have the chance to do what he wanted. He wanted to climb the ranks and lead. Chances are he won't live that long, so i assumed to let him do it now.

We made our way through piles of Afghan bodies down the halls of the capital building. Most of our guys that were wounded were in the library. So we made our way there. You could here gun fire and bombs outside but also crackling. Crackling from fire.

Jake glanced around a corner then stopped. He looked back at me with wide eyes. My heart dropped. What did he see?

I gestured for him to step back. He did so. I glanced around the corner. The smell flooded my nose even through my gator mask.

Afghan soldiers were standing around a few bodies. Pieces of bodies. And tossing them into a bonfire.

I turned back to Jake and nodded.

"Respirator." I whispered.

He ruffled his eyebrows.

"Trust me." I nodded. The smell would make him sick. He hadn't ever been around it.

He quietly hooked up his respirator. And we turned the corner firing. All six soldiers hit the ground. I looked at the bonfire and stopped.

"Go back." I shoved my hand into Jakes chest.

He stumbled back,"What? Why? We gotta go that way."

My eyes sealed on an American flag badge laying in the bonfire.

"Now, private!" I yelled at him. He responded and turned around and ran the best he could. I did the same. We turned the corner and kept running.

"Mary." I heard someone say. "Mary, come on." I felt someone rubbing my bare back. I blinked a few time. I was sitting on the floor. I looked up. "Hey." Rip rested his hand on the side of my face. "Ya alright?"

I nodded and breathed slowly,"Yeah. I think so."

There was a knock at the door. I jumped. Then looked up at Rip. "Go put a fucking shirt on." He helped me up.

I ran to the bedroom and heard Rip open the door.

"Keith took off." It was my dad.

I slipped on my shirt but decided to stay in the bedroom.

"What do you mean took off?" I heard Rip raised his voice.

"He's gone. The guys said he never came in after work. Have you seen Mary?"

I closed my eyes and prayed no one told my father what had happened.

"No, but we'll look for her. She's probably at the bar. I'll be down there in a minute." Part of me rolled my eyes, at the bar, really? It was believable but still.

And the door slammed. I sat down on the bed. Rip walked in slowly. And then he kneeled down in between my legs. He put a hand on my leg.

He sighed. "I told you to tell me-"

"I handled it." I cut him off.

He shook his head. His ears turned red and so did his neck. "Mary." He clenched his jaw. "Where is he?"

"The coyotes have him by now." I whispered. He stood up and grabbed his hat. He sat it on his head and started for the door. I stood up. "Rip, I had to-"

"No you didn't!" He turned around. He was pissed, as expected. "You can't do that shit around here anymore! Sheriff Haskell has his whole department on our ass. Any little fuck up and we'll lose this place. They're just waiting to take it." He shook his head and wiped his beard. "I understand it had to be done, but not by you." He walked up close to me and looked down at me. Back to the old Rip who was giving orders instead of having a conversation. "I handle that shit. Thats my fucking job. You don't do it for a reason. You're gonna get us caught doing stupid shit like that. You hear me?"

I stared up at him. He was a different man than he was maybe ten minutes ago. I clenched my jaw and nodded. "Yes sir."

I walked around him and out of the cabin. Slamming the door behind me.

I stomped down the hill and walked into the bunkhouse. Everyone stared at me when I walked in. Including my father.

"Mary..." He shook his head. Did they fucking snitch? There's no way.

"What's everyone's problem?" I opened the fridge and grabbed a beer out of it.

"Keith's missing. I don't want you going off on your own until we find him. Understand?" He rested his hand on my shoulder. He looked concerned. Like he cared.

"Uh yeah-" I swallowed, "Yes sir." I nodded. He patted my arm and walked out.

"So when do we tell him we're looking for a dead man?" Ryan opened the fridge and grabbed a beer.

"When we find the body." Lloyd grumbled and walked out. Most of the guys followed him, except for Jimmy who was sitting at the kitchen table.

"You killed him?" Jimmy looked up at me.

I nodded.

"Why?" He ruffled his eyebrows, "I know he was an ass to you and was always hitting on you but-" He shook his head.

"No one told you?" I sat down in a kitchen chair beside him.

"Tell me what?"

I sighed and took a long drink from my beer. "Keith worked here a little under 10 years ago." He nodded. I pressed my lips together, trying to figure out how to tell him. "At the time, there was group of ranchers that wanted some of our pasture ground. Dad didn't wanna sell it. They bribed Keith."

"With what?" He looked confused but also like he didn't want to know.

I stared off at the door. I blinked slowly, realizing I wish I would've never started telling this story. I felt a hole in my stomach growing and my throat started to hurt. "Me and Beth." His eyes grew wide. "He took us out of the house one night and brought us to them. He threw me out onto the road half way there. Decided he could only handle one of us. They tried to hold Beth as ransom for enough money equal to the land. Anyway, one thing lead to another and we both made it back home and now they're either dead or in jail." I shrugged. I left out most details. He didn't need to know everything. Beth and I told the story thousands of times to the cops when it happened that I never really wanted to go over it again.

"My god. You people never catch a break." He shook his head and started to stand up.

"Jimmy-" I grabbed his arm. He looked down at me. "Please don't say anything to my father. Deny everything you know. Play stupid. Lord knows you can get away with it."

He swallowed hard and nodded. "Yes ma'am- yeah. I mean no, I won't say a word. Swear." He babbled. I let go of his arm and he walked out the door.

I sighed and looked around the quiet and empty bunkhouse, something that was rarely seen. I slipped out of my jeans and into a pair of Nike shorts and a sweatshirt.

I laid down on my bunk and stared at the ceiling. I felt lonely. I was so use to being surrounded by people that it felt strange to be alone in the quiet. I wanted to be around my family. Kasey, Beth, and dad. And I would give anything to be with my mom. I think she would be proud of the strong women I am but she wouldn't approve of the violence I so heavily rely on at times. I couldn't blame her either. I know it's not ideal. Neither me nor Beth were the picture perfect ladies everyone expected us to be. At least Beth was able to run circles around a business meeting where I didn't even know what goes on in a business meeting. Maybe it was something I needed to learn. The business aspect of our farm.

I sighed and tried to turn my brain off but it kept running.

The door opened and slammed shut. I glanced over. It was Rip. I sat up and let my legs dangle off the top bed.

He walked over to me. He rested his hand on my knee. "You did good. He's already gone." He nodded and encouraged me as if it was a job I had been assigned even though he just chewed my ass out not even hours ago.

"I know." I nodded back with confidence.

"I shouldn't of yelled at you." His voice was raspy again. He was tired. "Just seems to be the only way you listen sometimes."

I huffed out a small laugh, "It's an army thing. Everyone yelled at me for years. Kinda just my language now."

He didn't break a smile. "You're not in the army anymore, Mary. You've gotta get that in your head. We've been through this a thousand fucking times."

I nodded. "Just a hard habit to break." I swallowed hard and ran my hands through my hair. From my roots all the down to the ends. It had gotten long since I came home and could actually take care of it. "Everything was drilled into our heads to show us how we survived..." I sighed. "Or tried to survive."

"You gotta talk to someone about what happened." He whispered. It was a matter of time before someone told me this. I was just waiting for it. And he wasn't wrong, but I didn't want to. The last thing I want to do is relive it. I want to get on from it.

But I just nodded, "Yeah."

20

"**M**ary!" Someone yelled my name.

I spun my horse around in the snow covered ground. It was dad. I sighed. I had too much to do today to worry about what he wants. I glanced over at Rip, as if to get his approval for me to leave. He gave a quick nod. I nudged my heals into my horse and headed in Dads direction.

"Yes sir?" I asked approaching him. He pointed his finger up and gestured to the ground. I swallowed hard and dismounted my horse.

"Put your horse up. Let's go the house." He nodded towards the barn.

I did as I was told but was anxious. My horses hooves clicked on the concrete floor as I lead him to the stall.

"Hey, Mary." Jimmy walked through.

I smiled at him,"Hey." He stopped walking and waited for me. "You need somethin'?" I rubbed my hands together to warm them up a little.

"Uh, yeah," he glanced at his feet then beside him and then finally looked me in the eyes,"Can you touch me to rope?" He squinted a little. The sun beaming off the snow and onto the concrete floor positioned itself directly to his eyes.

I tried to not seem excited but I definitely was. "Of course. Glad you wanna learn." I gave him a quick smile and walked away.

I made my way out to Dad and then we road the side by side over to the house.

I hadn't been in the house in months. It felt eire. He walked to his office, I followed. He sat down at his chair, I sat down across from him.

"You look terrified, Mary." He chuckled.

I tried to force a small laugh,"I am, sir."

His smile faded. "I know." He cleared his throat. "The night that..." He paused and shook his head,"That everything happened. Rip said there was a man who talked to you. Right?"

I blinked. Surprised Rip shared this with Dad. I guess I shouldn't be because I told the Sheriff everything. He easily could've told Dad too. I just didn't expect Rip to bring it up. "Uh, yeah. Yes." I nodded.

He stared out the window. "It was Jamie's dad."

"Oh." My eyes widened a little and my mouth slightly hung open. I was now even more surprised. Typically this was information I would have had to fight to get. Or found out in some extraordinary way. But no. He just told me. "Oh." I said again. "I never met him."

He still stared. "You did. You just don't remember him. Probably best you didn't. Anyway..." he readjusted and looked at me. "I think he was looking for a deed for some land-"

I wanted to roll my eyes. It's always about some fucking land.

"-and Rip can't find that deed. I had him keep a bunch of those papers a long time ago. I didn't think anyone would check his place for them but-" Dad stood up and looked behind his desk on some shelves. He pulled out a certain binder and opened it, flipping through the pages. He stopped flipping and pulled one out. "Here's a copy." He tossed it onto the desk. I leaned over and looked at it.

My heart thumped fast. "Is that the..."

"Yeah, it's the same land the Indians want for their casino." Beth walked through the doorway and grabbed the copy of the deed. She turned to a printer and started to copy the copy.

"So what's this mean? Why did he say you stole it from him?" I leaned back in my chair.

Dad opened his mouth but Beth started talking. "Because we did. Actually-" She handed me the new copy of the copy,"You did."

"What?" I furrowed my eyebrows. I looked down the bottom. Sure enough, my name signed at the bottom. "What the fuck is going on?" I looked up at Dad.

He pursed him lips together. "Beth couldn't be name of it because she's the attorney, Kacey couldn't because he's commissioner, Lee's dead, and I don't trust Jamie."

I stood up,"And I was in Afghanistan!" It was dated for three years ago. I wasn't here.

"I know, it sounds bad-" Dad said quietly.

"This is bad! If he's got that deed, how the fuck are you gonna explain I signed a deed when I was in the fucking desert?!" The paper crumpled slightly under my grip.

"I don't know!" He raised his voice. Then we were all three quiet. I swallowed hard.

I wanted to start in again about how I didn't want anything to do with the business. I just wanted to raise cattle. But it wasn't going to get me anywhere. It never does.

I glanced at the deed and then sighed. "Why'd we steal it?"

He wiped his face then sat back down. "Technically Jamie stole. During one of his many... many fuck ups, I asked him to have his dad write us for the land." He opened a desk draw and pulled out a bottle of Johnny Walker Black.

And two glasses.

He poured the liquor in both and sat one in front of me.

"And he did it?" I questioned then tossed the burning whiskey to the back of my throat.

"No," Dad did the same,"Jamie stole and forged it."

"And then you put my name on it?" I grabbed the bottle of Johnny and took a swig, then started to sit it back down. Dad motioned for me to give it to him.

"Yeah." He took a few swallows from it then put it back under the desk.

"So what... we just got wait now?"

He nodded. "Yeah."

Suddenly I heard the front door slammed. Rip quickly walked into the office.

"Sir, we've got a problem."

Dad opened the drawer and pulled the bottle back out.

21

"He did what?" I choked on my words.

Rip and I were riding across the pasture as fast as possible.

"He's fucking stupid, Mary." Rip shook his head. We approached a tree.

There Jimmy laid on the ground and Lloyd and Ryan beside him.

I jumped off my horse before he even stopped all the way. "Jimmy?" I jogged toward him. I hit my knees beside him.

I looked down at his leg.

"Hey." He said very breathy.

"Hey." I put my hand on his shoulder,"What happened?"

His eyes weren't focusing on me and he looked like he could fall asleep at any minute. "There was a bear."

"Yeah? Looks like he did a number on ya?" I motioned for Rip to hand me some of the first aid stuff we brought.

Jimmy was mumbling and jabbering.

I peeled back part of the shirt that was tied around his leg. I assumed Rip or Lloyd or Ryan had done this. It was smart to help slow the bleeding. A huge chunk of skin was in shreds on his calf and up to his knee.

"Is it bad?" He asked in a high pitched voice.

I put the shirt back and started to wrap gauze as Rip held his leg up from me.

"It was fucking bear, Jimmy. What the fuck do you think?" I sassed. "What in the fucking hell were you thinking?"

I kept wrapping. Just more and more, trying to stop the bleeding.

"Chopper should be here any minute." Ryan mumbled.

I nodded. Hopefully soon. He was loosing a lot of blood.

"I didn't want it kill the horses. They were tied up." Jimmy mumbled and lifted his head to look up at me. "Oh, dizzy."

"Hold still." I barked at him. "And don't fucking throw up."

He gave me a thumbs up.

I looked at Lloyd,"Horses were tied up?"

He nodded,"Had a tree down across the fence. Didn't even hear the bear or horses or anything with the chain saws going. Jimmy just happened to ride up on us. He tried to scare the bear with his horse but bear grabbed onto his leg and pulled him down. Heard 'em screaming when Ryan shut the chainsaw off. Never seen anything like it."

I swallowed hard and heard the thump of the helicopter. Rip turned his head to me. But I stayed focused and kept wrapping.

More and more.

"Just keep wrapping it. It'll stop the blood." I told one of the other privates who was wrapping Jakes leg or what was left.

I swallowed hard. And kept wrapping the helicopter was louder.

"What the fuck happened out there?" The private asked. I felt my eyes burn.

"He wanted to get everyone else on." On the helicopter.

The helicopter. It was loud.

I looked at Jimmy. It was Jimmy not Jake. Jimmy.

"Almost here, Jimmy." My voice shook a little.

"And we were almost there." My chest felt heavy. Hard to breathe.

I saw the black and yellow helicopter land a ways away. "Ya alright?" I asked Jimmy. He didn't answer.

"Is be okay?" I mumbled. "Jake?" I grasped his shoulder. The private shook him too. It started to rain. And thunder.

"Jimmy?" I hollered at him. I glanced over and watched as Rip met the medics halfway and followed them to us.

"He's not responding." The private shook his head.

"No." My mouth was dry and my face was wet from the rain. "He was just fine."

"Is he responding?" The medic asked as he approached.

My mouth hung opened. "Uh, no. Not now. He was..." I got dizzy. Hang in there, Mary. "He was just fine."

"He's lost a lot of blood." Ryan spoke up.

And then packed him up and took off. I walked unsteadily to horse and got on.

"Mary!" I heard Rip try to call out to me over the sound of the helicopter.

It started to sprinkle rain. I ignored him. I wanted to be alone. I wanted to be away from everyone and everything. I took off towards the mountains. Leaving everyone else in the dust.

The sound of the helicopter in the distance was getting louder. "They're back." I whispered. "We gotta get him to the bird!" I hollered to the private.

"Corporal they won't take him. He's gone." The private said softly, rain covering his face.

I tightened my jaw. "He's fine. He's lost a lot of blood. He's just unconscious."

"We'll never make it back to the landing zone! They got a full force between us and them!" The private shook his head. "It's over, Dutton."

"He's not dead." I whispered. "He's going home. You're going home. They'll cut us up and burn us in a bonfire then roast marshmallows over it if we stay. Take him and go through the embassy. I'll distracted outside. I'll cover you. No matter what you see or hear. Keep going." There was a lump in my throat.

He nodded. "What if they want to leave as soon as we get to the chopper?" He already knew the answer. But he wanted me to tell him it was okay.

"Don't worry about me." I gave a small smile. "I'm too stubborn to let hadji roast marshmallows over me. I'll be there, kid." I patted his shoulder and off he went.

The next four minutes felt like an eternity. I threw grenade over the wall and fire bombs on the inside of the wall. I ran for my life and hid and shot at tens of men. I had hand to hand combat at one point. But it all happened so fast I couldn't be sure what was going on. I just trying to get through to the other side. I heard the chopper close by. The propellers were loud. They were very close.

I watched as the private I had just spoke with minutes later ran from the embassy and to the chopper. I smiled and started to head that way too. I tossed another grenade in the opposite direction to draw away attention but it didn't work. They saw me run to the chopper. Soon bullets whizzed by my head. I turned around and began to shoot. Not taking too long to aim for anything. Just holding the trigger and praying I didn't run low on ammo. I held them off and back stepped to the chopper. Someone grabbed my pack and was hauling me up into the chopper as it started to rise. I was still shooting. I felt my ass hit cold metal and my leg sting suddenly. I still shot.

"You can stop, Corporal. We're in the air."

We were in the air. I nodded. And smiled. I turned to Jake.

He was pale. My smile faded.

"Jake?" I shook his chest. The medic on the chopper pulled him from us but I could see everything. They ripped the bandages from his leg. And the leg just crumbled to pieces.

My eyes burned. "Jake?!" I grabbed his arm. He didn't answer still. "What's going on?" I asked a medic who turned to me as the other one tried putting him on oxygen.

"'Corporal, you've been shot." He said.

"Me?" I looked around. My leg. It hurt. "Oh." I closed my eyes.

I opened my eyes. It was raining. And I didn't know where I was. Just in a pasture.

22

White. Everything was white. It was clean. I hadn't seen anything this clean in a few years.

Beep. Beep. Beep.

I looked to see where the noise was coming from. To my left was a machine with my vitals, hooked into an IV in my arm.

I tried to sit up. I grunted as pain shot through my left side.

"Corporal." My staff sergeant stepped into the room. The hospital room.

"Sir." I nodded.

"How are you?" He asked.

I was taken aback. Not prepared for this question. This wasn't a question they trained you to answer like most. "I'm okay, sarg."

He nodded. "We need to talk about a few things. And this isn't going to be easy."

I gritted my teeth and stared at him. "How many?" I whispered.

"Mary, that isn't important right now-"

My throat had a lump in it, "How many... did we lose?"

He was silent. Then he opened his mouth just to shut it again. Then he spoke. "The Land was killed. And five from your platoon." My eyes burned. For fucks sake Mary, don't cry in front of this man. "Private Martin... Jake-" My jaw started to shake a little. "He wanted to tell you he made it home. But..." He cleared his throat. "The plane that was bringing him and other passengers into the states was hijacked."

"Oh, god." I felt like I was gonna throw up.

"He over powered the hijackers but died from the injuries sustained during it. The plane landed safely. He's being awarded a Purple Heart. His family wants you present for the ceremony." Sarg cleared his throat after spilling out the news.

I took a deep breath. "Okay. When- when do I get released? I can fly there and back within a couple days-"

"'Mary, you're going home." He cut me off.

My heart shattered. "Sir-"

"You're injured. You've been shot in the leg. You're not gonna walk the same for a while. Go home. Be with your family. You've done your part." He turned the walk out. But he paused. "You did a hell of a job, corporal. No one else would've held that Embassy as long as you did. You're an amazing soldier. Your country is proud of you." He pointed to the TV on the wall.

Sure enough, my picture scanned the screen, along with news coverage and photos of the embassy take over. The title of American hero flashed on the screen.

I dropped my head. And sobbed. I didn't feel like a hero. I felt like I failed.

I glanced at the phone by the bed. My shaky hands picked it up. And I dialed the only number I could remember.

"Hello?" The voice rang through on the other end.

"Rip? It's Mary. I'm- I'm okay."

*****

I opened my eyes. I was looking up to the sky. The clouds were dark and the sky was getting there. My mouth was dry. My head hurt. But my horse and I were huddled under an old cedar tree. It had the most coverage from the rain so I assumed that's why I had been under here. But my clothes weren't wet. And neither was the ground.

I stared out at the mountains and the streams in the mountains and the trees surrounding the streams. I breathed heavily. My stomach rumbled. Something felt off.

I looked up at my horse. He was staring too.

"Pretty view, isn't it?" I asked him. He moved his big head to me then back out. I sighed. "I failed." I whispered. "I was suppose to get everyone home alive." My eyes teared up. "I wasn't suppose to be the one coming home. It should've been me. He was suppose to go home. Hell, he had a whole life in front of him. He was gonna do great things. Better things than I'm doing here." I wiped the tears from my eyes. I sighed again. Jake would love it here. The mountains and the cold. He loved the mountains in the desert but hated the heat.

Soon I heard thumping in the distance. A horse running. It got louder. And soon, the horse and a cowboy popped over the hill.

"Mary?!" Rip yelled but he didn't see me. I stepped out from under the cedar tree. He's head snapped in my direction. He dismounted his horse quickly and jogged my way. He opened his arms. I was taken aback but I didn't care. I wrapped my arms around his neck and squeezed. I buried my face into his neck. He held me right to him. "What the hell were you thinking?" He pulled me away from him and held my shoulders tightly.

I didn't have an answer. Not right away. I didn't know what to tell him because I didn't know what I was doing. I felt lost. Scared. Pissed. Overwhelmed.

"I'm not suppose to be here." I said softly.

"Fuck, no, you're not suppose to be here. This isn't even your land." He was still stuck in his seriousness. He wasn't understanding what I was saying.

I didn't wanna say these words. I didn't know how. All I knew was that it was going to make me feel weak and I hated that feeling like I've said thousands of times before. But I needed to. He was right all those months ago. I gotta make peace with what's left.

"Rip," I whispered,"I'm not suppose to be alive."

The anger inside him quickly faded. His tight grip on my shoulders loosened and he let go for a second, shocked by what I said. Then he put his hands but softly this time and gave a gentle squeeze.

"Mary..." He shook his head,"You can't think like that."

I stared into his brown eyes. "It's all I can think about." My voice still hushed but cracking now. I hadn't ever said it out loud. "I don't want to be here. I shouldn't be here. It's not fair." I felt my body weaken. Rip was staring at me so closely. Like he was just as terrified as I was. "I lost soldiers over there and I'm suppose to come home and be okay. They had families, Rip." Tears started to pour from my eyes. "I didn't have anybody. That's why I was good at my job." I raised my voice a little. My job. God I miss my job. I was good. It was the only thing. I was ever good. at. "It was okay if I didn't make it. I took risks that everyone else wouldn't." I stepped back from his grip. "And then the discharged me. They said I did great and better than anyone else would've. That our country was lucky to have me. And then they got rid of me!" I yelled, tears streaming down my face now. "I wasn't done! I should've went back! My whole life was out there and they fucking ripped it away from me." I swallowed hard, causing myself to gasp after. I clenched my jaw hard. In this moment, I hated everyone and everything. I wanted to scream and hit something. Anything. "I want my life back." I whispered and let my arm hang by my sides. I didn't have to energy to pick them up.

"Mary," He placed a hand on the side of my face. My vision was blurry through tears but I stared at him deeply. Please tell me what I want to hear. Tell me to go back. If he tells go I'll fight to go back with everything I have.

But it wouldn't be peace. It would be more hate. You tell me to find peace. I'd do whatever he told me. My eyes begged him for the answer. Tell me what to do. Where is my peace. How do I get it. I'm done thinking for myself. Please tell me.

Tell me to stay here. Stay and here and live with you. My heart started shattering. I would only stay here for you. Let me be here with you and start a new life. One without war and death and blood and tears and hate and violence. One with love and family and friends and cattle and the ranch and with you. God please tell me this.

Tell me we can be fix this. That my pain isn't permanent and that these flashbacks are over. That I can stop reliving my past because you're going to show me peace. And that it's all over. No more missions to kill people. Only Sunday mornings drinking coffee and Saturday nights playing poker at the bunkhouse. Only moving cattle and fixing fences. Training new cutting horses and helping baby calves survive. Bottle feeding and keeping them warm. That these attacks on the ranch is almost over. That we find what they want and just give it to them. And that you're gonna keep me safe through it all. You're going to show me a whole new side of you that I only get to see ever so often. Let me see it all the time. Let me see the gentle and loving you, because that's where my peace is. That's where I find it. That's how I'll heal. Tell me that's how I can heal.

Tell me that I can love you. Tell me I'm allowed to feel safe around you no matter what my father thinks. Tell me you're going to fill and fix these holes in my heart from losing my mom and Lee and Jake and the Land team and the men from my platoon with love and care. That love and care is going to in my life everyday because of you. Tell me you want to marry me and start a family. That we'll build a bigger cabin together and it'll be ours. Tell me this is my new life. This is my peace. This is where I find peace with what I have left.

For fucks sake, Rip. Please tell me this.

23

H e didn't tell me this.

He didn't say anything.

It wasn't until after my next two deployments that I was fully able to find peace. Our last mission to assassin the Taliban leader, was successful. We thought maybe the war would be over soon. Just a few more months and every one could go home. All the gunfire and fire fights around us, we picked up what we had at our site. And planned to take it back to base to start on a new mission, somewhere. I learned later on they were going to send us to Russia. Thank god we didn't, I would've hated the cold.

My buddies and I loaded the last of the medical equipment into a chopper and it took off. It was just us in our little site. At least twenty miles from anyone else. We would leave out in the morning when the chopper came back to get us and our tents.

That night after we ate and drank together, and played some poker, I sat outside my tent and stared at the mountains. The mountains.

I bet Rip was watching the mountains from his front porch. What I would give to be sent there right now. To be back go those nights we would sit and talk and drink on that porch. How peaceful it was there.

I stopped thinking. Peaceful.

It was peaceful. I stood up.

"Guys, I gotta home." I said out loud to my fellow soldiers. They looked confused at first.

"Are you done?" One of the other corporals asked.

I pressed my dry lips together, chapped from the desert sun and wind. "Yeah," I let out a deep breath,"I'm done."

*****

The small black car pulled up to the gate of the ranch and started to drive up.

"Stop here." I spoke up to the driver. He stopped and I got out. I slung my duffle over my shoulder and started walking up the long driveway.

It was a cold October, colder than the first time, and although I layered on my jeans and sweatshirts and vests, I was freezing. Once again, I was still use to Afghanistan's desert heat.

I looked around me and soaked in the Montana view. I missed it. I actually missed it this time. I missed the smell of the snow on the mountains, it smelled like rain. I missed the sound of the wheat and Johnson grass swaying and the whistle of the birds. This is my home. And I was sure this time that I'm staying. Home to stay.

I could see the cabin. It was early. He should be stepping out any minute. And he did. I walked faster. I dropped my bag onto the ground and quickly stepped up the porch steps.

A smile broke out across his face. He sat down his coffee cup as I grabbed his face and pressed my lips onto his.

His lips were warm and soft and made me feel like I was a whole new person. I leaned and deeper into him. His arms engulfed me as he kissed me back.

"Did you find your peace?" He asked between kisses.

"Yeah," I pulled away and moved my hands down to his chest. "It's here." I patted his chest.

"Good." He kissed my forehead. "Because I love you. And I don't want you to ever leave again."

I smirked,"Yes sir."

He shook his head but broke into a smile. I giggled but was soon cut off with his lips pushed against mine.

I was glad to be home. And I wanted to be home. I wanted this is be my home forever. So finally, I found my peace. And I was finally home to Yellowstone.